TIDE
WATER
TALISMAN

TIDE
WATER
TALISMAN

by
Glynn Marsh Alam

MEMENTO MORI MYSTERIES
New York

Memento Mori Mysteries
Published by
Avocet Press Inc
19 Paul Court, Pearl River, NY 10965
http://www.avocetpress.com
mysteries@avocetpress.com

Copyright ©2010 by Glynn Marsh Alam

AVOCET PRESS

Library of Congress Cataloging-in-Publication Data

Alam, Glynn Marsh, 1943-
Tide water talisman : a Luanne Fogarty mystery / by Glynn Marsh Alam. -- 1st ed.
p. cm.
ISBN 978-0-9725078-9-9 (alk. paper)
1. Fogarty, Luanne (Fictitious character)--Fiction. 2. Women detectives--Florida--Tallahassee Region--Fiction. 3. Tallahassee Region (Fla.)--Fiction. 4. Talismans--Fiction. I. Title. II. Title: Tidewater talisman.
PS3551.L213T53 2010
813'.54--dc22
2010025035

Cover photo: Camy Keele

Printed in the USA
First Edition

AUTHOR'S NOTE

The fictional location for this book is somewhere along the north Florida coast where the Ochlockonee, St. Marks, and Apalachicola rivers meet the saltwater of the Gulf of Mexico. The Palmetto River, which is central to all the Luanne Fogarty novels, as well as the St. Margaret are composites of the many rivers that flow in the area.

I want to dedicate this book to all those who live and work on the Gulf of Mexico. Your fortunes and misfortunes are well noted. And to all those who are working hard to save the sea life and marsh animals that are threatened there.

Charming the storm didn't work the year of big hurricane Katrina. Neither did riding it out in the manner of years past, when folks taped up windows, nailed shutters, and prayed to whatever deity was at hand. The winds and tides wouldn't quit. Nor would the floods that ran over the levees and tore down the shacks, whiskey parlors, chapels, casinos, and voodoo niches. Some say whole stashes of jazz instruments ended up in the Gulf, along with gambling tables and farm animals from on up the coast. People navigated makeshift boats into the Gulf, heading wherever dry ground greeted them. Others swirled and drifted with the currents, and finally met their Maker in the depths. The storm claimed its booty. The water didn't care how it got it.

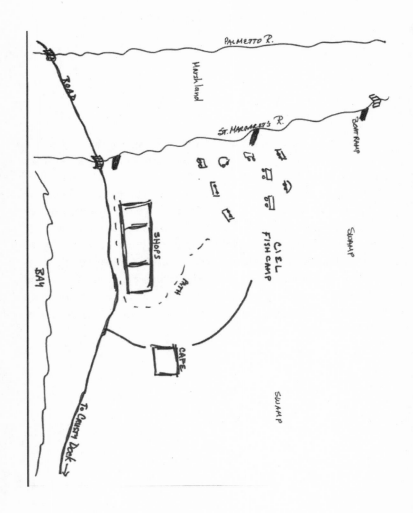

CHAPTER ONE

I hate death in any form. Even the natural kind where the aged person dies at his prescribed time, during his sleep. It leaves a hole like when a trusty old fence post is jerked from the ground. The hole has to gradually fill up with dirt and leaves until we have all but forgotten it was there. Dorian Pasquin has had a few holes to contend with this past year. Two of his swamp buddies, old men who were younger than he, came to the end of the river, as he put it. He didn't seem to mourn much, but a quiet pall comes over his leathery face at times, and his old man drone goes quiet. The semester had ended in June, one more year for me in the linguistics department, and I was using the extra time to be with him more, to draw him to the living, and maybe to make him laugh, the day we headed for the fish camp by the bay.

"Old man, don't you do any sharp turns with this boat."

Mama, the proprietor of Mama's Table, wasn't one for riding in boats on a river. She shifted her hefty hips onto a seat in Pasquin's motor boat. She held on to a stuffed, broken, loose leaf binder packed inside clear kitchen wrap and held together with a thick rubber band. It was her restaurant guide, as she called it. A collection of regulations and recipes.

Mama tucked a floppy hat onto her permed hair and tied its strings at the top of her neck. The bow disappeared beneath folds of chin fat where the skin was as clear and smooth as it was when she was a baby.

"This old man don't do sharp turns, woman. You just sit still and admire the scenery." Pasquin's leather face turned toward the open river. He nodded to me.

I sat in the seat beside Mama, ready to pat her chubby arm should she go hysterical if the wake of another boat gave us a sudden lift. We headed for the bay where we planned to meet up with some Katrina refugees. Not refugees anymore. They had all come to this area in the days after the big hurricane in 2005, escaping jammed up shelters and polluted waters, not to mention a government that didn't bother much with a rescue effort. New Orleans made the biggest news, but the destruction was just as bad along the Mississippi and Alabama coasts. Not a single one had anything left to return to, so they stayed. From the Louisiana Creole to the casino worker from Biloxi and the fisherman in Mobile, they used what they could scrape together to build up little businesses and buy small boats.

"Are you sure you know the way to the Shrimp and Chevrette?" Mama seemed to enjoy saying the name of the new café, like it was some exotic first class establishment instead of something that amounted to saying The Shrimp and Shrimp Café.

"Know it," said Pasquin, his chest heaving an impatient sigh even though we couldn't hear it over the engine.

"We'll stop at the bridge, just before we hit the bay. I got some stuff to pick up from a bait shop there." Pasquin didn't face Mama when he said this, but from the side, I could see his mouth turn up in a sly smile. He knew she hated riding in boats. Waiting in one docked near a busy river spot wasn't going to soothe her fears.

"What's he got that you need?" Mama's big face scowled and turned red.

"Wants me to take some equipment to one of the shops in

Ciel." Pasquin referred to our destination in the term coined by the ragtag refugees who had settled near a rundown motel. Amongst the coastal pines there, on land owned by a local tree farmer, sat the ruins of the Heavenly Motel. In the 1950s, people rented the rooms to get away from their small town life and fish in the salty waters of the bay. But as times got better, they opted for condos on St. George Island or at least modern trailers parked closer to the bay bridge. The Heavenly Motel decayed more each year, its bright blue and white sign crumbling until the words were barely readable. When one of the Katrina fishermen, desperate to locate cheap housing, saw the place, he brought others there. He used his Cajun French, combined it with English, and called it The Ciel. Soon, everyone not only called the motel ruins by that name, they referred to the entire refugee settlement in the same way. Some of the inland natives who wouldn't know a Cajun or a Catholic were surprised to see it written C-I-E-L. To them, it should be See-Ell or even Sea-L.

"Will they have enough customers to run a café there?" I asked Mama to turn her attention away from griping at Pasquin.

"If the food is good, and the word gets out, they'll not only have their own people. They'll get lots of fishermen and people from the fish camp. The women who follow their men to those camps on vacation don't really want to get stuck in a hot trailer frying the catch of the day." She nodded her head, causing the floppy brim to nod with her. "They'll have customers, all right." She patted the binder. "Provided it all tastes good."

"And it don't provide them with the ptomaine," said Pasquin. "You best read them people the laws about hand washing and stuff. Have themselves sued before you know it." He tossed the rope to someone standing on the dock and tipped his straw hat at the man when the boat was secured. He turned and winked at me.

"I saw that, old man," said Mama. "Just get your tail back here and let's get round the bay before some big storm starts to shoot lightning out of the sky."

"Such a scaredy cat," he chuckled. "Look at me. I been on this river for years and ain't been struck once."

"Listen!" She shook a chubby finger at him. "I don't like the idea of being seared. I prefer to do that to meat or fish. Now hurry up!"

Pasquin made a sweeping bow with his straw hat, slammed it on his head and trudged up the bank to a concrete structure.

Mama made a tiny growling sound in her throat, gazed up to the sky that was still sunny, and eased back in the boat seat. I patted her hand and smiled.

"Now what does this family want you for?" I asked, more to take her mind away from the imaginary impending lightning than for information.

"Kayleen has been wanting to start her own restaurant ever since they decided to stay," she said. "She's been hauling herself out of bed and traveling nearly twenty miles to work at a seafood place in Carabelle. Bub has been working boat mechanics the whole time and couldn't help her out. I guess they finally saved up enough money to start something where that old café used to be."

"Bub? What a name," I said and closed my eyes.

"Kayleen says he's been called that so long he forgot his real name. He even wanted the preacher to use it when they got married." She giggled like a little girl, but her bulk bounced the boat in tiny little jerks. "Preacher wouldn't do it. Said it had to be legal."

"That was back in Biloxi, right?" I knew it was. The origins of these families had been told to us all many times on my own front porch and in Mama's Kitchen over plates of fried mullet. They had lost it all in Katrina and had accepted the welcome aid from towns along the Florida part of the Gulf until things could be straightened out back home. Some had lost just too much, or maybe never had enough to lose, and had found somewhat of a haven in the little fish camp down from Carabelle on the bay. When the camp owner said they could use the crumbling motel structure, they did what humans do—let their dire condition become the mother of invention.

"Not exactly in Biloxi, little patch of a town outside. They never had much then. Bub was a boat and car mechanic, but he couldn't stop them boats from sinking to the bottom of the ocean after they'd crashed against some trees. Kayleen already worked in a café up near I-10. She's put in her training time and ought to know the secrets to running a good café." Mama patted the covered recipes that rested in her lap.

"You aren't going to give her your recipes?"

"Some. The ones that are well known already. She's most likely got some of her own. What I got to make clear to her is the legal stuff that could get her into trouble if she won't pay attention to them."

"Like food poison?" I knew the results of too much heat, humidity, standing fish, and unclean cabbage for slaw. It had hit me too many times in tiny joints along this part of the coast.

Mama nodded. Then she shook her head. "Can't understand how owners can let it get that far. I catch any of my help not washing their hands, I'd swat 'em with some tongs."

"You would, too," I laughed. "So, is that all you know about Kayleen and Bub—prior jobs and silly names?"

Mama balled up a fist, threw out her index finger and shook it at me. "Now, Luanne Fogarty, don't you be rude. These people haven't had it easy. Not even before that big storm."

"Sorry," I smiled and kept quiet. I knew better than to start a defense argument. Rude was rude.

Mama eased off again and shaded her eyes as she looked at the sky. Thunder rumbled miles away.

"Lots of old stories came out of those coastlines and bayous," she said. "Kayleen told me about how Bub met her and tried wooing her right from the start. He was like some kind of wild man out of the swamps at first. Took a lot of grooming, she said, to make him presentable enough to marry." Mama hiccupped a laugh. "Some women just got to marry somebody no matter what it takes."

I looked at her and raised my eyebrows without saying a word.

"Okay. I know I did the same, but didn't take me long to realize I wasn't going to keep a 'cause' around the house even if I was married to it." She sighed. "Kayleen couldn't help it, I guess, and it seems to have worked out. We'll know after this café gets going."

"The Shrimp and Chevrette," I smiled and tried to picture some farm boy trying to explain to his friends about this good place to eat down on the coast. Chevrette was likely to turn into some kind of General Motors car before long. "Kayleen must plan on making some Cajun delights as well as Southern seafood," I said.

"Yep," said Mama. "She says she got lots of old Cajun recipes from places around where she lived. Hot stuff." She shook her head. She never had tried cooking it herself, but she imported some sauces from New Orleans and allowed people to ruin the cornmeal fried oysters with burning stuff from a bottle. Pasquin was her best customer there.

"You may want to advise her to change the name of the place," I shifted and tried to sound humble with my suggestion. "I mean, *chevrette* means shrimp in Cajun French, but how many Cajuns do we have around here? Most locals who took high school French are going to look it up and think *little goat*. Doubt she'll be serving that."

Mama frowned and shot me a wrinkled brow look. She shifted on her seat and said nothing, but I was sure she'd pass along the information to Kayleen.

A "whoeee" sounded from the top of the bank. Pasquin gripped one side of a large crate, and someone he had picked up at the bait shop had the other. Whatever was inside looked heavy and metallic. "Hold the boat steady, Luanne," he shouted as he and the other fellow edged down the bank. For a man in his eighties, Pasquin's feet kept a remarkably steady grip on the loose soil.

"What in the world?" said Mama as she held onto the seat with both hands. Her face went pale when I pulled the crate aboard and made the boat rock.

"Makes espresso coffee," said Pasquin. "Kayleen bought it used from somewhere, and they delivered it this far." He shoved the crate into a secure corner and dropped into his seat. The boat bounced, and Mama let out a little scream. "Don't worry, woman, I've just got to sit down a minute and rest these old legs." He pulled out a handkerchief and swiped his face a few times.

"See ya, Pasquo," said the man who had helped him.

"Pasquin—and thanks. Don't know where old Jimpson is. He said he'd be at the shop all day."

"No note?" I asked.

"None. Except the one on top of this thing. Says I'm supposed to pick it up for Kayleen Romaine."

"Well, you done that. Now, let's go," said Mama, still holding her seat with one hand.

A noise without expression emanated from deep in Pasquin's throat as he pushed the starter and turned the boat away from the dock. His little vessel that provided him about as much mobility as any car looked overloaded with three humans and a crated espresso machine. Maybe the added weight would help control the bounce as we headed into the open bay. It was only a short distance to Ciel, but Mama wasn't going to care for swells and wakes from other fishing boats.

Pasquin guided the boat along in his slow silence, barely making his own wake and turning away from any faster ones nearing our side. He seemed contemplative, inside himself, rather than one with the elements as he usually was. He had pulled the old straw hat firmly on his head so that only the brim moved in the wind. His banter with Mama was normal. I knew something else was bothering him.

"Where did your friend, Jimpson, get off to?" I took a chance that the missing bait store owner was perplexing him.

"Not like him to go away and not tell anybody," said Pasquin, his voice low and barely audible over the engine noise. "Door was locked. Guess he had some emergency."

"Does he have relatives around here?"

"Never said." Pasquin looked into the distance, his head shaking. Jimpson would have been one of his late night buddies, the ones who stopped by for some bourbon and raw oysters and stayed up past midnight, talking away the old days on the river, maybe making fun of some old coot who drank himself silly and ended up on a cypress knee. Pasquin could count off the number of times he rescued someone from a night with snakes and gators and a bed of pure mud. Most of these pals knew each other's history and would know if any relatives lived close enough to call in case of injury, or even death. If Jimpson had never said, then there was no one around he'd be visiting this time of day.

"Could be somebody lives out of state," I said. "Somebody got sick and he had to run."

Pasquin shook his head without saying anything.

Mama looked at me and shrugged her heavy shoulders. She only knew Jimpson as a customer every now and then. She frowned and turned her face to the shoreline. Our silence could feel the worry on Pasquin's mind.

"Ciel coming up," he said. "Heaven is the next stop." He turned the boat into a small cove lined with the pines that grew along the sandy shore. At one point, a wooden pier darted into the water, far enough out to dock small boats like Pasquin's. From where we sat, we could see the boards lead to a road that was wide enough to slide a fishing vessel into the water. Beyond that, the pines thickened again and we could only see a hint of the little row of shops and would-be café.

"How you going to get this machine all the way up there?" said Mama.

Pasquin smiled and attempted to retrieve his humor. "Thought you could pull it with the boat rope."

"Hmpf!" That was all Mama could say as she put out her hand to slow the boat's movement next to the pier. She never actually touched a board, but it was a mental reassurance like someone pushing an imaginary brake on the passenger side of a car.

"I'm calling on the cell phone," I said. "Kayleen said they'd send someone with a truck."

The truck, with its four wheel drive and extra cab, came with

Bub driving it. He parked above the boat ramp and tossed a cigarette out the window.

"I got a dolly," he yelled, and pulled it out of the bed. "You bring the boat closer to the ramp and we'll get everybody out." His bristly face and skinny bowlegs matched the chain smoking. Years of outdoor boat work had rendered his skin the color of a bad leather tanning job. But his strong arms could still grab heavy equipment and yank it to dry land.

"Not a light thing, this machine," said Pasquin. He guided the boat close to the water's edge where Bub leaned over and with both hands, forced the crate with its espresso maker out and to the ground.

The sudden jerk forced the boat to dip, then rise, with a suddenness that drew a whoop from Mama. Her wrapped recipe book fell onto the bottom of the boat.

"If that had hit the water…" she began and decided not to continue with the threats in front of a new café owner. Instead, she held out her hand to Pasquin who helped her rise and exit the boat. I held it as steady as I could by leaning in the opposite direction. "Oh, I am happy to be out of that thing," she said as she stood on the ramp.

We piled into the truck, Mama in the front with Bub, Pasquin and I in back. The espresso machine rested between the dolly and a fishing tackle box in the flatbed.

"Had some activity going on at the camp last night," Bub pulled out a cigarette, took one look at Mama and stowed it behind his ear. "Gibby's been at his nightmares again. Got so loud somebody called the law. Took them 'bout forever to come, so Miss Doucet's boyfriend went stormin' over there and threatened to bounce Gibby's head right out of the park." He slowed for an intersection where four dirt roads merged with pines on all corners. "Should have, too. We don't need some ol' drunk skunk waking us up at night."

"And how much does Carol Gibson need Gibby beating up imaginary demons every weekend?" I asked.

"Must do," he said. "She stays there."

I sighed. Carol and Gibby had survived Katrina, but the forces that got into his head during an all-night stay in waist high water had turned him into something who saw bullies and giant snakes all at once. Carol, his wife, had been in Arkansas when the storm hit. She landed back in the state within ten days, but it took her nearly three weeks to locate her husband in a shelter. There was no house to return to, so they accepted a ride to the Florida coast and set up in a little trailer. Gibby had been quiet for most of the trip. At least until he settled next to a man who owned a shrimp boat and offered him a job. The man had the habit of downing a bit of rum after a load had been dropped off at the dock down by the bay. Offering Gibby a gulp had been the beginning of his "heebie-jeebies" as Pasquin put it. "Brought out all the fears of drowning in rising oily water," he told me once as he sat in a rocker on my front porch. "He had to fight off some people who grabbed hold of him. Some say he watched a kid drown in that dirty levee water. Been fighting ghosts ever since—with a little help from the bottle."

"Where does he get the booze?" I asked Bub, who was bouncing his truck too fast down the dirt road. Mama held on, one hand on the grip over the window, the other against the dash board.

"Can't say." Bub didn't offer anything else, and I wondered if he wasn't a sly supplier.

"Does he still go out on the shrimp boat?"

"Yep. Long as he's sober, he's quiet and knows what to do."

Bub's hand reached behind his ear. He pulled it away as though realizing he'd have to wait until we arrived at the park before he could pull a long drag.

"How come you're not passing the shops?" asked Mama.

"Took the short cut to the trailers. We got to pick up Kayleen." He turned and grinned at Mama, his tobacco stained teeth a mixture of yellow and brown. "She won't have nobody going in that place without her there." He smiled and turned onto another road that led into the back of the trailer camp where both refugees and locals lived year round. "Nope. Nobody's going into that café without Kayleen's invitation."

When Bub slammed on the brakes in front of a round top trailer, we eased out of the high cab, grateful for the stillness. Kayleen stood in the doorway, grinning from a face that was still pretty after years of living with Bub. She had what most people up north described as Southern alabaster skin, still smooth and moist without makeup. There may have been lines, but they were plumped out with a bit of weight that had always been there. Dark, curly hair surrounded her face and set off blue eyes. Her grin showed white teeth. She had never taken up the habit of smoking.

"Pretty as ever, Miss Kayleen," said Pasquin as he tipped his hat her way.

"I brought the book," said Mama. She stared at the small steps that led into the flimsy trailer. It wasn't a place she wanted to enter, and her face showed the same apprehension she had at entering Pasquin's boat.

"Just leave it in the truck," she said. "I'm taking some other stuff to the café and need Bub to help me load it."

Mama spied a lawn chair and headed toward it. "Then I'll just have a seat out here and wait." She smiled, relieved at a problem solved.

Pasquin found another chair under a tree and pulled it next to Mama. He fanned himself with his hat while she batted at mosquitoes. Bub followed his wife inside where they fussed about this set of dishes and that set of pans. It was time for me to drift, to explore this place that I'd seen only once before when the Katrina group was deposited here. The local Red Cross had found the spots for a lot of them, but it was this small group that stayed. The others had long gone home to repair their broken lives.

I walked through a pine lane and passed small trailers tucked into clearings. The occupants had filled them with belongings too cumbersome to stuff inside their tiny living quarters. Outdoor grills that saw frequent use stood in the elements, going rusty in the salt air. Boats, some on stands, some resting on dirt, others on carriers, filled spaces between trees next to the trailers. I wondered if the people ever really used them. Not many people were visible, but I could hear them inside the trailers where they escaped from the heat. Most had air conditioning units hanging from a window. An elderly couple sat under an awning they had placed on one side of their trailer. Both dozed but opened their eyes and nodded when I passed. The woman's wave consisted of two fingers going back and forth with a final double flip. It threw me for a second, like some kind of sign a kid would make.

The trail ended at the edge of the river. I could see the open bay at one end. A few yards down was an old boat ramp that the trailer owners could use to go into the river, but I figured most would prefer the newer one farther back, the one we had used. I gazed across the water. The river was wide here and the other side wasn't too clear at first. I shaded my eyes from the sun and focused on a dock with a ramp beside it. A familiar-looking boat tied up there.

"Action over there, it seems." Pasquin made me jump. I never heard him coming. "Sheriff's boat." He nodded in the direction of the opposite shore.

"Yes…," I said and let my thoughts drift. Vernon Drake, my love and comrade in swamp crime as he called it, had been away for over a week. Some case he couldn't talk about, he'd said.

"Coming out of the woods," Pasquin nodded again. He had removed his straw hat and used it to shade his eyes.

"You see pretty good for an old man," I said.

Two uniformed deputies emerged from the thick growth of pines and oaks. One went onto the dock and began waving at a boat coming from upriver. It was another sheriff's boat.

"Amado," said Pasquin. "And he's got Sergeant Loman with him."

"Vernon won't be far behind," I said.

That's when a group of men came out of the forest. Two carried a stretcher with something covered in black. It didn't take much to realize it was a body. I held my breath and squeezed my eyes shut. I hadn't heard from Vernon in a while.

"You can open your eyes," said Pasquin. "There's your fellow."

CHAPTER TWO

There's nothing like the feeling of dread turned to relief. Being part of danger was in Vernon's job description, but I knew I'd never be prepared to lose him this way. A tall man with a shiny bald head, still in his diver's suit, appeared like a hero in a dream from the pines. Another diver followed close behind. I moved closer to the water's edge where I would be visible to those on the other shore. I saw Tony Amado look my way for a moment, long enough to know he recognized me. He was the head honcho over there, the lead detective in whatever they were trying to solve. He turned away and stood near Vernon. He must have whispered something because Vernon turned around suddenly and stared my way, nodded and turned back. He wasn't going to risk waving.

"They got a body," said Pasquin as two deputies loaded the tarp-covered lump on the stretcher into the back of one of the boats.

"Is there water on the other side of that group of trees?"

Pasquin paused for only a moment, then nodded. "A lagoon shoots off the bay and surrounds a clump of land. Not enough land to build anything and probably too soggy anyway."

"But the water is deep enough to drown someone?"

"Ma'am," Pasquin used a term that was affectionate when I was a child, but tended toward sarcastic now. "If your nose is down, you can drown in an inch of water."

I nodded. Vernon would get in touch as soon as he could, but given his silence these past days, I knew the operation was secret—not to mention his whereabouts.

"Hey!" Bub hollered from a few yards behind us. "We're ready to load up and go. I'm taking Kayleen and Mama and about half the kitchen in my truck. Carol Gibson will drive you two in her jeep."

"Jeep?" said Pasquin. "Too hard on the bones." He shook his head but walked back to the trailer-park with me.

"What's happening over there?" Carol asked as we approached the ragged piece of mobility that had seen more than its share of brambles in the forest. "I've watched boats go back and forth from across the way about all morning." She didn't mention the deputy's car that had visited her place and calmed Gibby down enough to let the neighbors sleep.

"Not sure," I said and climbed into the back seat. I left the front for Pasquin. It had more grips.

"Where's Gibby?" Pasquin changed the subject. He knew better after all these years of giving information to law enforcement than to speculate on what we saw.

"Sleeping it off," said Carol. She frowned and looked toward her little trailer. "He fought the demons out here last night. Staggered around and shot his fists all over the air. You'd think ghosts from the depths had risen up just to haunt him."

"More like ghosts from the bottle," said Pasquin, more to himself than to Carol.

Carol picked up a paper sack full of cleaning products and plopped it onto the seat beside me. Behind me, were more paper sacks with what looked like napkins.

"Let's go. I want to be here when he wakes up. I got all the booze out of the house, but he's got a knack for finding more."

I took a lesson from Mama and grabbed hold of the side and the back of the front seat as we bounced through the trees on a rutted road. Carol knew her way, but didn't much care that we'd get butt bruises from riding like this. With the way she revved the engine in places, I could feel the anger that rose inside her. She had demons, too, and it didn't take alcohol in her system to bring them to the surface.

Pasquin's leathery face winced a few times before he grabbed his straw hat from off his head and slapped it on his knee.

"How are the other shops doing?" He yelled above the grinding gears and engine noise.

"So-so, I guess," said Carol. "Mo's store always does good because people would have to drive five miles to buy toilet paper if he wasn't here." She didn't brake for a dried up mudhole and the jeep swerved enough for her to jerk the wheel away in time to keep it from hitting a pine trunk. I heard a whispered curse from Pasquin. "And old Har-Har isn't hurting none with his junk shop, either."

I smiled. The use of shortened names had its place among this group. Mo was Morris, a transplanted card dealer from a Biloxi casino. He was the first to clean out an old motel room and put in general goods that any convenience store would stock. Weekend fishermen who ran out of beer could trot over and grab a six-pack instead of storing it a cooler or worse, in valuable trailer fridge space. Along with gum, candy, and cigarettes—not to mention toilet paper—he probably pulled in a steady income.

Har-Har wasn't really a name anyone called Harold to his face. It was meant to be nasty and to describe the kind of stuff he had on hand to sell. He was from Louisiana but didn't know a word of Cajun French. His family had been farmers, so he said, but somehow the farm was gone long before Katrina blew water over it, and Harold himself had called a jail cell home for a few years. He had dealt in junk before the storm and knew how to do it here. He was the first to clear out two of the motel rooms and fill them with discarded boat parts, old tables that had escaped the ravages of termites, and assorted tools that needed the rust scraped off them during his spare time. He had plenty of that. People would rummage through his crowded stock and come up with an old hoe or maybe a tackle box. They'd find Harold in his cane chair and ask the price. He'd guess at it, pocket the money, and send them off happy. Then it was back to the slow scraping. Rust oil lay on one side of the chair and a soda can on the other. Carol and the others thought his place a laughing stock and began calling him Har-Har in private. He was a silent man, and someone who could give a cold stare without a blink. They didn't try calling him that where he could hear them.

"Guess that little Marci is doing her thing, still?" Pasquin was prying now, looking for swamp gossip. He'd find out a lot more when he nosed around the places, but he needed his background. He's the reason I knew so much. On long nights that began at sunset and lasted until the stars came out, we'd sit on my porch and rock. Iced tea, lemonade, or the occasional rum and pineapple drink would keep his throat wet as he told the stories of how these folks lost it all—and that wasn't much—along the Gulf coast in '05 and what they did when the local government offered them places to stay here.

"Little Marci Doucet will always do just fine, thank you," said Carol. "Anything goes wrong, she can just call on one of her voo-doo gods or meditate or tell a fortune—whatever. She thinks the spirits will guide her." Carol slowed the jeep a bit. "Hah! Wish Gabby would grab hold of her kind of spirits and leave the rummy ones alone."

Pasquin forced a chuckle. He glanced back at me and lifted his eyebrows briefly. "She's got a lot going on in that place, yes ma'am."

Carol finally hit a wide grated road and then a gravel one. It lead to the clearing where the old motel stood. The shop owners had cleared the parking lot of broken concrete and scrub, had it grated off and covered with more gravel. Anyone driving here could park and walk along a cobbled sidewalk in front of the shops. Mo's Convenience Store occupied one end, Harold's Oddities the two middle spaces, and Marci Doucet's Talisman at the other end. Beyond that, sitting two car widths away, the old motel café had been renovated with paint and new glass. A delivery truck waited outside to put some tables and chairs ordered from Tallahassee into the place. Kayleen didn't want booths. They were too expensive, she said. The building was now a bright aqua, to match the ocean was the excuse I heard. Thankfully, no name had yet been painted across the wall.

"I told her what you said about naming it the Shrimp and Chevrette," said Mama. She fanned herself with the recipe book and waited for Kayleen to open the door for the delivery men. "She's giving it some thought."

Bub gripped a lit cigarette with his lips and began helping the delivery men. They unloaded the boxes, he cut them apart, and together they moved them inside the building. Kayleen had marked off the new vinyl floor, taking care to measure exactly how much room would be between each one. When the boxes with the chairs came open, we all helped, primarily because we were dripping in sweat and wanted to be inside to experience the new heat pump that sent cold air through the vents.

"Dear me," said Mama as she ripped open a long package of plain white napkins. "I'll smell like a donkey before I get home.

Have to shower before serving."

She didn't wipe her face for long. The call to check out the refurbished kitchen pulled her behind the swinging door. Kayleen's café was a lighter blue than the aqua outside, but it maintained the ocean theme—or rather the fish and seafood theme. Shell décor had been added to the walls on shelves set high above the tables. They were real shells, she said, shellacked to keep them from corrosion in the room with cooking oils and bright lights. She had installed some pocket lights in the ceiling but made it clear that only the candle lamps would shine on the tables at night. When she pointed to the row of lamps—fashioned like something you'd see on a nineteenth century vessel—I took that as a signal to keep up and help. I took one of the wipes from a plastic container and handed both to Pasquin.

"You wipe each table top with a separate cloth. I'll put the lamps in the center."

His grunt was audible, but he pushed himself to his feet and began the process.

Dishes and cookware came from cartons in the kitchen and sat haphazardly on shelves, inside cupboards, and in drawer. Everything shook in rhythm with Mama and Kayleen yelling over the din.

"Got to tell them women they can't talk that loud when customers are here," said Pasquin. He turned around in search of a trash can, finding an empty box to use instead. "They planning on having any music in here?"

Bub, collecting empty boxes, heard him. "Yep. Got a new player and a system to pan it out here. Not sure yet what we'll play."

"Some Cajun music, some zydeco, maybe?" I winked at Pasquin. That would have been his choice.

"Country, too. Maybe some rock 'n roll oldies," said Bub. "We got some CDs at the trailer. Thought we'd get some music from Miss Doucet, but have you heard that stuff she plays?"

"No, but I'd like to." I placed the last lamp in the center of the last table and admitted the place was coming to look like people could eat fried shrimp here. "You want to check out her place?" I said to Pasquin.

He chuckled. I could tell he'd been itching to get inside The Talisman since we passed its dark blue walls with something that looked like wispy women painted in white.

The Talisman was, in a way, a cliché. It seemed out of the 1960s or maybe the later New Age movement. In fact, it just about included all the movements one could think of as long as they had occult, magic, Eastern or spiritual tied to the description. Marci Doucet was of French decent, she said. She also said she owned a Creole shop in New Orleans before the storm, not by herself but in partnership with a real Creole woman who knew the old voodoo. She bragged about how much that woman had taught her but never said what happened to her, only that their shop had been washed away. It took her a few months to redo this one room of the motel and stock up on esoterica, but once she got it going, the inhabitants of the trailer camp would drop in when they got bored with their checkers and fish stories to sniff the burning incense, buy some "French" soap and maybe a book or two on how to cast a spell. She had bragged lately—so Kayleen said—that she was getting clientele from the tourists now and some down from Tallahassee.

"Got some ghosty things on the walls," said Pasquin as we opened the door and passed beneath a sprite with a bell.

Inside, the odor of mixed incense, candles, and perfumed oils engulfed us like an ether. I went light-headed for a moment. Miss

Doucet had placed a small ceiling fan in the middle of the room, and it wasn't until I stood beneath it that my head cleared.

"Many aren't accustomed to the oils of the spirits," said a soft female voice from behind a counter. At first, I couldn't see anyone, just boxes, figurines, and nonstop candles. Miss Doucet's dress was constructed of some ethereal-looking scarf material, mimicking the colors around her. Her face and hair were nearly the same beige color. If she hadn't moved, she would have looked like something painted there.

"I guess I'm not," I said. "It's a bit overwhelming."

Pasquin winked at me. I knew he was thinking more along the lines of stinky, rather than spirit, scented. He stood next to a bin of toy snakes, their movements made easy by joints every inch.

"Almost look real, don't they?" He said. "Colors and everything."

"Who buys them?" I asked.

"Sometimes we get children in here who want them, and gardeners say they keep squirrels from their flowers. Mostly they go to people who want to cast symbolic spells." Miss Doucet pointed to a rack of books behind the snakes. "We do a lot with casting spells in here." She smiled and looked down at the counter, a movement more to prove her serenity than in any kind of bashfulness.

I nodded. I knew it would take those squirrels about one hour to figure out the snakes weren't real, and I knew the spells wouldn't work, real or symbolic, or however it might be done. Police work had ruined any kind of belief in such a world for me.

"The name of this place is The Talisman," I said. "Do you carry any?"

Miss Doucet smiled without showing her teeth and moved from behind the counter. Actually, she stepped down as her place seemed to be a platform built up to look over the store. She wasn't tall, and her small bones draped in that scarfy material made her look even more fairy-like.

"We have lots of information on our talisman objects in the store, if you'd like to read about them." She picked up a few pamphlets and pointed out some hardback books. "The more common ones are in these bins, but we have some quite valuable—and I'd like to add, powerful—ones in the cases." She raised one small hand like a ballerina to indicate some artifacts in wall cases. "Just let me know and I can unlock them for you." She smiled and nodded at us like a queen and returned to her throne behind the counter.

I drifted around the room with Pasquin. He picked up carved ogres and small broomsticks, chuckling like a devil who mocked such things.

"She's got the act all sewed up," I whispered to him. "The gestures, the dress, the colors—everything you'd expect to see in a place like this."

"Think she flies home at night?" He said.

"On fairy wings, for sure. Right to her trailer."

We had moved to the back when the sprite over the door tinkled her bell and a drab woman in shorts came in with a mesh beach tote. Her straight pale hair draped around her face in thin whisps, and her elbows and knees looked like bones poking from thin poles.

"Miss Doucet, how are you today?" Her voice had the roughness of a smoker, and she followed her question with a slight cough.

"In calmness," answered Miss Doucet. "You're a little early but Sheila will be here soon. I feel her presence already."

"I wanted to shop for some salts," said the woman. "The last are about gone, and they make my skin feel better."

"Yes, they would." Doucet moved her scarfed body from behind the counter once more. She stood for a moment, almost like posing, next to large glass bins of substances. In an ordinary store, they would have held candy or nuts to be ladled into plastic bags. She pulled out a fancy paper bag from below the bins and opened up one with white crystal looking stuff.

"White to purify aging skin that has seen too many negatives," she said and began dipping the salts into the bag with a clear plastic scoop. "Be sure you use them in a clean bathtub at least once a day. And say the blessing over the water prior to getting in." She folded the top, placed a sticker on it and returned to the counter to do the very nonspiritual thing of ringing up the bill.

"You know," I whispered to Pasquin, "if she had told me I had negative aging skin, I'd have decked that woman."

Pasquin chuckled. He motioned to a sign above a door in the back. **READINGS BY SHEILA**. Doucet had turned a closet into a fortune telling room.

On the other side of the back wall, the owner had placed some photos. One seemed to be a small shop somewhere else, maybe the one in New Orleans, and another was a shrimp boat with its name painted on the side, TALISMAN. I wanted to ask if this was a relative and if other members of her family were so into the spirit world. Before I got up the nerve, the sprite at the front rang again and in walked an elderly lady in a flowing muu-muu that covered a hobbling body. Her white hair showed off a ruddy skin that made her seem younger than the rest of her.

I sidled close to Pasquin. "That's the lady from the trailer-park. She was sitting next to a man and gave me a funny greeting."

CHAPTER THREE

All three women gave the Indian prayer bow to each other, tapping their lower chin with the finger tips of folded hands.

"Give me five minutes, and I'll be with you," said the woman whom I took to be Sheila. She hurried past us into the room reading room. "I'm late because of some activity across the river. I need to clear my aura."

"Something happened on the river?" said the woman in the direction of Sheila, who had slammed the door behind her.

"You mustn't allow negatives into your space now. Keep yourself clear for the reading. If the river has anything to do with you, Sheila will know."

The woman's worried face emphasized the deep leathery wrinkles. She had been on the water for years from the looks of her.

"Would you care to see our new amulets?" Marci Doucet was at the woman's back before she knew it. "They just came in from bayou country." She waved her arm in a magic wand gracefulness toward a wooden box the size of a kitchen sink. "Haven't even had time to unwrap them."

The woman followed the hand movement toward the box and peered into the depths. She began to pick up cellophane and tissue-wrapped baubles.

"Anything to ward off water monsters?" the woman's eyes pleaded in Miss Doucet's direction. "I just know something has happened on the river. Feel it in my bones."

Marci Doucet placed a gentle hand on the woman's shoulder. "Not your bones, your spirit." She made a frown to match the woman's. "That spirit needs cleansing." With a glance toward Sheila's closed door, she picked up a cloth bag from inside the amulet box. Opening the drawstring, she let a round, iron ball fall into her palm. Holding it up with two fingers, she peered through the carving of the hollow amulet. "It opens, you see, and you can place the blessed herbs inside for better protection." She pulled on the clasp until it finally gave and showed an empty space inside. "Wear it on a chain or carry it in your pocket, but make sure you place the correct herbs inside if it is water protection that you need."

I watched the woman turn the small bag over and look at the tiny price tag. She scowled a bit when Doucet picked up a clear bag of nasty looking weeds and offered it to her. I figured she was about to be scammed and headed her way.

"Excuse me, but I couldn't help but overhear what you were saying about the amulet." Before Doucet could regain her composure, I leaned over the large box. "Why are some in cellophane, others in tissue, and a few in cloth bags?" I rummaged with my finger.

"Please!" said Doucet as she shoved the box a bit to one side. "They will be taken out for display as soon as I can get to them." She stopped, and like some robot who needed a button pushed, changed her expression to the angelic fairy again. "I'll be happy to explain." She turned to the box and pulled up a cellophane wrapper. "These have limited ability. Most are made from simple, cheaper materials. The ones in paper are a grade higher, and the bagged ones are of high quality, and carved, thus allowing more protection."

"I see," I said. What I really heard was that more money meant more protection. Not much different from the world of criminal gangs.

The poor lady had watched this exchange and had discreetly placed the iron amulet on the counter. She was edging her way toward Sheila's door. Doucet saw her and stepped her way.

"By the way," I said. "Just what is the difference between an amulet and a talisman?" I waved her attention to a glass case hanging on one wall. It was just enough time for the woman to move behind a rack of Wicca books, out of Doucet's line of sight.

Marci Doucet took time to stop and smile sweetly at me. She waved that gentle palm at me like an Ahab waving to his sailors to follow him to the depths. I followed. Pasquin met us at the wall case and gazed into the clean glass.

"A talisman from this box has great powers," Doucet said. "They have been endowed with that power by various shaman and priestesses from many places. If you notice, they all come with a chain, but some work best carried in a pocket or favorite purse."

"So they are only for women?" I loved playing dumb at times.

"Why, no. Men use them, too." She frowned for a second, withdrew a key from her pocket and opened the glass case. "Please look all you want, but I must ask you not to touch. Their power is best when touched only by the owner."

The door sprite rang the bell and a man walked inside, his khaki slacks and polo shirt on a lumpy body made him a tourist—or at best an outsider not a fisherman. Miss Doucet gave us a smile and nod and went to greet him.

"Looks like a lot of polished shell stuff to me," said Pasquin. "She never did answer your question."

I turned around to a book rack and pulled off a book about talismans, amulets, and other charms. "Maybe it will tell us here."

Pasquin pulled the book toward him. "Must not be *talismen*, then," he chuckled. "Talismans just don't sound right."

"Says here that an amulet is something that has power in itself, while a talisman has to be consecrated with power." I looked up at the case. "Okay, that piece of tin has been consecrated with power to do what?"

Pasquin moved close and squinted. "Looks like somebody carved it up like a shrimp. Maybe it's got the power to pull in a boat load." He glanced around to see Miss Doucet's back turned toward him, and reached up to touch the object. "I'm pulling out the powers, I guess, but I see something carved right around the head of this shrimp." He ran his thumb over the piece. "It's a cross. A holy shrimp." Before I could answer, he began to stifle his own chuckles. "Didn't that priestess know you pull the heads off shrimp before you eat them?"

I was about to join him in some silly giggling, when I saw the new visitor pull out a wallet with an ID in it and flash it toward Miss Doucet. I heard a soft "over here" and watched them both go behind her counter.

"This could be good," I said. "You stay here." I moved slowly toward the front of the store and stood behind a tall counter of books. Behind me was a display of crystals, each with an explanation of their powers. Miss Doucet could see the top of my head but not much more, and I hadn't spotted any security mirrors in the store. I turned my back and began reading the crystal labels.

"I've been hired by the Guerrin family to find out what happened to their cousin after Katrina." The man wasn't shouting but he didn't try to lower his voice.

"I have no idea what happened to Janine," answered Doucet in a low voice. "The shop was gone after the flooding and so was she."

"You were her partner, so the relatives say."

There was a pause, and I was tempted to turn around and watch the expression. "No. Janine owned the shop. I was like Sheila back there. I rented a room in the shop and read Tarot cards for customers."

"Then you had no financial interest in the shop?"

"Only what I made from the readings. Even the table and chairs were hers. I did have a few packs of cards and a table scarf that were lost in the water. Other than that, I got out with my life."

"Fair enough." I heard the man walk into the shop. "Nice place you have here. Is it anything like the one in the Big Easy?"

"Yes, I suppose so, except I may be a little more broad in my merchandise. I believe in many of the cosmos religions, you see. They all have their own blessings."

"And Janine Guerrin?"

"She was more inclined to the islands. She was Creole, you see."

"Yes. I've met just about all the family left in Louisiana. It's kind of urgent they find her."

Silence filled the shop. Whatever Sheila was reading out of the poor trailer-park woman's palm was done so low that it didn't pass through the flimsy closed door. Pasquin stood very still before the talisman case. I figured he'd picked up on the conversation, too.

"Ma'am," the man said, "where did you go during the hurricane?"

"Oh, I took refuge in a school shelter up in Mississippi. I'd heard the storm was coming and got out of there. Drove northeast as fast as possible. Janine said she'd go to some relatives in northern Louisiana."

"But she didn't give you an address where you could meet up afterwards?"

"No. And it was quite a while before I went back. The shop was nothing but clutter and mud and broken stuff by then. I had no idea where she was and I sure wasn't going to leave a note in that place. Then, my brother told me about the camp here."

"Your brother?"

"Yes, he works the shrimp boats. He was off Texas when the storm hit and took refuge inland. I found him through the company he was working for at the time."

"And where is he now?"

"Why, here. I mean he lives with me when he's around. Mostly, he's on the Gulf. Captains his own boat now."

"Things got better for you, it seems."

By this time, I had turned around and was staring at the man between books on the rack. His dark eyes were sheltered by thick eyebrows, but the hair on his head was thinning, so much that soon it would not exist at all. I watched him swipe a handkerchief across his mouth and forehead. It was too warm in the shop, but Miss Doucet had busied herself lighting more incense. She smiled at his sweat.

From where I was standing, I could see outside the window if I looked around the display of candles and carved totems. Someone was coming at a fast pace across the sand beyond the walkway.

"Vernon!" I said under my breath. He was out of his diving

suit and had put on his deputy uniform.

I slipped from behind the cases and headed for the door, knowing the sprite would chime, but I didn't care. I met him before he got too far from the shop.

"What's going on?" I said, falling in step beside him.

He stopped abruptly. "I was looking for you. Thought you'd be at that excuse they're going to call a restaurant." He took a look up at the sign over Miss Doucet's shop. "You're buying fortune telling stuff now?"

"Just humoring Pasquin. It got pretty boring folding napkins."

"Where's Pasquin?"

"Inside. Why?"

He didn't answer, just took my arm and walked me back to the front door. It chimed as we entered and all three inside looked up to see the uniform enter.

"Ma'am," Vernon nodded his greetings. "Just looking. Not here on business."

"And I do hope you never have to be, deputy." Miss Doucet smiled like a cobra this time. I was already thinking of finding a snake stick. "Are you interested in the occult arts?"

Vernon was clever. He just smiled and began to wander about the place. He nodded at the private detective—or at least that's what I thought he was. The man nodded back, grabbed some herbal soap and said, "I'll take this."

I was grateful. Miss Doucet would have to refocus her attention to the sale. Vernon and I walked to the back. Sheila's door was still closed.

"You get close enough to that door and you'll hear some weeping," said Pasquin. He held onto a small bag. "I bought something. Had to if I wanted to stay in here long."

About the time the detective left the front door, the woman

came out of Sheila's door. She was dabbing at her nose with a crumpled tissue. Her eyes grew wide and she nearly ran to Marci Doucet.

"I want to buy that amulet with the herbs now."

Doucet returned to the box and fished out the bag with the iron amulet and grabbed the herbs. She passed them under her nose and then under the woman's as though proving they were the real thing. I wondered how much essence oil was on the wilted leaves.

"Do you want a chain, too, or would you prefer to carry it in your pocket?"

"Not in my pocket. I might forget it. I'll get the chain and wear it all the time."

She pulled bills from her purse and Doucet rang her up, placed the goods in a bag, and smiled. She had that smile down to an art. It tossed away any argument.

"Feel free to return for more herbs if you feel these are getting stale," she said.

"Stale?" I whispered to Vernon. "The things are dried, dead as corpse. How can they get stale?"

Vernon didn't smile. He took my arm and nodded towards the door. "Let's get out of here," he said. He gave Pasquin another nod, letting him know he was to go, too.

We walked toward the restaurant. Inside, we found Mama sitting at one of the tables with a glass of tea and her recipe book. She was underlining some things in red.

"I made copies of some of the food laws and I'm giving these to her. If she ever makes people sick, she's going to lose a lot of business. Maybe get closed down. Best to avoid that right from the start." She glanced up at Vernon. "Don't see you dressed like that everyday."

"Who's here?" he asked.

"Just me for now. Kayleen needed some stuff from the trailer and made Bub drive her there. Not sure where Carol is. Was she supposed to come back for us?"

"Good," said Vernon. "Let's sit down." He pulled chairs out for Pasquin and me, then placed himself in the fourth one. He took a quick look at Pasquin. "There's bad news."

The table grew quiet. Mama's raised pen stayed in that position and Pasquin's old eyes went from shock to acceptance before anyone said anything.

"It's Jimpson, right?" He nodded to himself.

"Yes," said Vernon, a bit relieved that this old man could read just about anything in the swamp. "We found him inside his shop, in the back area where deliveries were made."

"How?" said Pasquin.

"Looks like something hit him over the head."

"Or someone?" Pasquin's eyes never watered, but the depths of them took on a lethal glow.

"Could be. It doesn't look like a box fell on him or anything like that."

"His door was locked," said Pasquin. "He didn't answer, and I had an inkling something wasn't right. Who could lock that door?"

"Anyone," said Vernon. "It just had a little catch to press. Whoever was in there last could have done that."

The silence at the table frightened all of us. A merchant, an antiquated one at that, a swamp dweller who had a wide range of others who would have defended him had they been there, was dead. Not from some snake or alligator who might be doing what nature intended, but by another human hand.

"Vernon," I said. "If Jimpson was found inside his store, who was that you pulled out of the bayou?

CHAPTER FOUR

Vernon didn't know who the dead man was, and he didn't feel the need to discuss him at the moment. He kept glimpsing at Pasquin and frowning.

"You'll be all right, Pasquin?"

Pasquin nodded slowly, his eyes revealing nothing but heavy thoughts. For all anyone knew, he was leveling the odds of walking through a snake-filled forest at midnight instead of mourning over a lost friend. I knew better, of course, but death was something different for him, something that happened if you didn't play the game of the swamp. Death always got you in the end, but not before you put a few out of your way first. That few was usually some dangerous animal or natural storm, a tide or maybe a mistake in that dark forest. He must have had a difficult time of weighing murder.

"Any idea what happened?" Pasquin's voice stayed low and even.

"Not yet, but we need you back at Jimpson's place."

Vernon had a sheriff's boat and offered to transport him, but Pasquin insisted on taking his own. He wasn't going to shirk his duty with me and Mama, either. We'd go back the way we came. Vernon nodded. He knew the old man needed his familiar comforts right now.

"You go on," he said. "We'll follow."

I made a quick call to Kayleen's trailer to tell her we wouldn't be there when she and Bub returned. Mama would leave her some notes in the kitchen.

This time, Mama didn't complain about climbing into the boat or scream when it rocked and tilted under her weight. Her face grimaced, and I could tell she was holding her breath. When she finally settled on the seat, bound book on her lap, she said, "Okay, I'm ready to go." In happier times, she would have called him "old man."

The ride into the bay, and past the two rivers that opened their contents to it, went silently. Mama grabbed hold of the boat's side a couple of times, but she said nothing. I took the cue and stayed quiet, too. Pasquin held his gaze to the river and ran the usual steady pace from the rougher bay waters to the calm of the Palmetto River. The wind as well as the water calmed here and we rode like travelers with Charon over the Styx until we reached the bridge. That's where we met the police boats and deputies standing by patrol cars on shore. Even from where we sat, we could see the yellow tape blocking off the few spectators along the banks. It was late in the day, and most fishermen had loaded up and pulled their boat trailers toward home. Only a few locals who might have sat and had a beer with Jimpson after a long day throwing nets for mullet stood around with long, frightened faces.

Vernon waved Pasquin on by and pointed to a place to tie up at the dock.

"Tie it up tight," said Mama. "I don't plan on getting out unless the sheriff says I have to."

I followed Pasquin up the hill to the spot where Tony Amado stood with Sgt. Loman. Both were pacing while a forensics team worked inside the small bait shop. I knew Marshall Long would be there somewhere, thankful he could do his work on land even if he had to reach it in a boat. The steep bank would have been a problem for him and his heavy bulk. Most likely, he came the long way around in one of the patrol cars.

"Maybe you'd like to sit on one of the benches," said Tony when Pasquin joined him. He pointed to two old bus benches Jimpson had found somewhere and placed outside his shop. It would have been ideal for old men to sip beer and swat gnats, talking about river feats of long ago.

Pasquin took a seat and fanned himself with his hat. Tony and Loman sat on either side, filling up the bench and most likely producing sweaty thighs where they touched. Vernon and I sat on the second bench.

"Tell me about this morning," Tony said. "How did you find this place?"

Pasquin said nothing more than I already knew. He had knocked on front and back doors, tried to see through one small window in the back, then commandeered a young man to help him with the crate that was sitting out front.

"Did you notice any disturbance, like footprints or blood near the back door?" This would have been a bit strange for anyone else, but Tony knew Pasquin would have seen something unusual like this. His keen eyes picked up more than most would in this forest.

"Nothing that looked like a scramble in front or back. No blood. Just locked doors."

"And Jimpson wrote the note on the crate?"

Pasquin looked puzzled for a moment, like he was trying to remember any handwriting he'd ever seen from his friend.

"I don't think so," he said. "You'd better get your lab guys to check, but I think that note came from the seller, or maybe the people who delivered it here."

"Any idea who that was?"

"Check with Kayleen Romaine. She'd know who she bought it from, and maybe they'd know who delivered it." Pasquin suddenly looked sad and shook his head.

"Who were Jimpson's enemies?" Tony tried hard not to be matter-of-fact, but to add some sympathy to the questions he asked of someone who had helped him out more than once with swamp people.

"Enemies? I don't think Jimpson had any. Not now. Maybe when he was twenty." Pasquin smiled. "Had lots of girlies back in his day."

"Then I'll need a list of people you think were his friends, visitors and such. If nothing else, we have to rule them out." He shook Pasquin's hand and nodded to Loman to write down whatever Pasquin gave him.

"You got any ideas?" I asked Tony as he motioned Vernon and me to join him near a huge oak that threatened to topple into the river with the next hurricane feeder band.

"Robbery, I'm guessing. Somebody caught him off guard, knocked him in the head and locked the doors when they went out. We're hoping for prints." He turned to glance at the building where Long and his team dusted and scooped up evidence. "The body is still there. I hate to ask Pasquin but he needs to identify him."

"You mean no one else can?" I figured anyone who fished on the river would be able to do that.

"I have to use someone reliable. He's it."

"Any weapon found?" Vernon asked.

"Not yet, but Long says it's probably a tree branch. He spotted splinters in the scalp wound."

I didn't know Jimpson, had only heard Pasquin talk about him and their river adventures over the years. From the glimpses I'd had of him, he was about the same size and had the leathery skin of someone who had lived that long under the sun and wind of open boats. He probably had the same natural instincts of river creatures and swamp dangers that Pasquin did, and drank the favored bourbon along with lots of beer. Was he a little plastered when someone decided to bonk him on the head?

"When did this happen?" I asked.

Tony shook his head. "No one seemed to remember the shop being open today. At some point the crate turned up outside the door. Long will have to give us a better idea of time."

He looked around when Marshall Long emerged from the back door of the shop. His white lab coat flew open in the late afternoon breeze. Marshall, a tall man with a bulk that gave him the look of a moving earth machine, pulled out a handkerchief and swiped it across his forehead as he approached us.

"Well, if it isn't the tadpole twosome," he said, referring to Vernon and me. "You think something could be in the water?"

"Time of death, Long," said Tony. He was a man of little humor or patience when it occurred on a case.

"Can't tell. Somebody left the AC on in there. A cold body won't tell you things like that. You need to find somebody who's been in the store today, or at least who saw him recently." He looked around and spotted Pasquin. "I'm ready for him."

"Let me," I said. I walked to Pasquin and asked if he was up to identifying his friend's body.

"Hell, yes," he said. "I want to see exactly what some bastard did to him. Then we're going to find the snake." He stood without the hesitation he usually had when he placed his weight on his old knees. "Lead the way."

I nodded to Marshall who took Pasquin's arm and guided him to the door. I followed, hoping Tony wouldn't stop me. I wasn't on a case unless he asked me to dive, but this time he left me to look after Pasquin.

The old man didn't need looking after. I suspect he knew pretty much what he'd see and was ready for it. Marshall leaned over the scene tarp and pulled it back far enough to see Jimpson's face. I had stopped in the doorway, but I had a clear vision between Pasquin and another scene tech. Jimpson's face had turned a deep color, almost like over tanning. Thick rusty blood rested on top of his head, the obvious spot of the wound. His mouth and eyes were partially open.

"Yep," nodded Pasquin and turned toward Marshall. "That's old Jimp. Why's his face that color?"

"We found him face down. Blood settled there. We've turned him over."

Pasquin nodded but didn't move until Marshall dropped the tarp over Jimpson's face and guided him back to the door.

"Who found him?" I asked.

"Off duty deputy was down here to go fishing with his kid. He needed some bait and couldn't get Jimpson to the door. Tried calling him on a cell phone. No answer. Figured something was wrong and just pushed open the back door. The lock wasn't worth much."

"Must have been a real treat for the kid," I said.

"He'll have it all over his elementary class for show and tell when school starts."

"Can we leave now?" said Pasquin. "I want to call a confab and see what the swamp rats want to do about this."

Tony had joined us and frowned at that comment.

"Don't go vigilante on us, old man," he forced a smile.

Pasquin stared at him without a grin or chuckle. "I'm talking about a funeral. He won't have any relatives. It's up to us to arrange things."

Tony fidgeted and stared at his own shiny shoes. Marshall rolled his eyes at me. We both knew Tony's people skills were still in development, or maybe had ended there.

"We'll let you know when the body will be released," said Marshall. "You can go ahead and talk about what to do but don't set a date yet."

Tony raised his head. "We'll have to look for next of kin even if you think there isn't any."

"He may have some," said Pasquin. "Just couldn't stand them."

"Was anything stolen?" I asked more to relieve the tension growing inside Tony.

"Maybe some change in the register," said Vernon, who recognized Tony's dilemma. "We aren't sure if he even took in any money today."

"All right," said Tony. "You're free to go." He turned toward Pasquin. "And thank you, sir. Let me know if any of your mutual buddies have any ideas."

At any other time, Pasquin would have come back with another quip to further annoy Tony, but this time, he just nodded and put his straw hat on his head.

Mama was dozing and sweating when we returned to the boat. She awoke with a start when Pasquin pulled the tie closer to the dock.

"Finished?" she said. It was an obvious question, one that was really asking what the hell happened up there.

"Totally finished for Jimpson," said Pasquin. Bitter sarcasm wasn't his style.

Mama looked at me as I climbed in beside her. Her eyes were

wide and frightened.

"Murder," I whispered. "Someone knocked him over the head with a limb."

Pasquin took us slowly down the river. Even in what should have been rage for him, he never pushed the boat to full throttle. It was as though he had to move with the currents, to let things come to fruition in their time.

We passed a grove of cypress trees, their knees poking far above the water's surface daring any boater to race and not pay attention to the dangers there. Moss draped from the high tops of the trees, and above it, vultures gathered for the evening treats they thought they'd find on the river bank. Shadows gathered around us, and for once, I was glad Pasquin would be home before dark.

"We'll have a river funeral," he said. "We've all been talking about what we'd want since Mr. Death seems to have graced our swamp this year. A river funeral to strew old Jimpson's ashes where the bay begins."

"He wanted that?"

"Yep. Cremation and strewing on the river. That's what he wanted."

"Then he's not Catholic?" I knew Pasquin had a partial Catholic background, but he never did anything about it or the other half of the family that left him a Baptist tradition.

"Not anything to my knowledge."

We drifted on, and Mama clung to the side of the boat even though the water ran smoothly now and other boats had abandoned their outings to tie up at docks along the way.

"By the way," said Pasquin. He bent down and pulled out the bag from The Talisman shop. "I bought you something today."

I opened the bag, staring back at him in bewilderment. I expected something funny, a joke gift that had been forgotten in the seriousness of the moment with Jimpson. I unwrapped a chain with a cross-studded shrimp at one end. The whole thing had been polished into a rusty gold color.

"It's a holy shrimp," he said. "Wear it for protection around water."

CHAPTER FIVE

Pasquin told me to wear the holy shrimp all the time. With death in the air, as he put it, I needed all the help the stars had to give. I put it around my neck before pulling myself off his boat at my landing. He saluted and headed for the tiny town of Fogarty Spring where he would help Mama get up the dock steps and into Mama's Table in time to shake up her help for the evening meal. I knew what Pasquin would do then. Unlike many men, he wouldn't sit in the dark with drink in hand to brood on the unfairness of life and drift into a drunken oblivion. He would gather his swamp denizens about him—I was betting that most knew about Jimpson already through some magic communication amongst the low-growing scrub and the high cypress. They would have drinks in hand for most of the night. They'd talk about their friend and his years on the river, but they would intersperse the tales with speculation and anger about his killer. By morning, they might even have a suspect or two, but no one would say a word until they checked it out themselves. Such was the way of people who chose to live here. The law had been too far away to exist for them in their youth. Now, they lived without it as much as they could.

I turned toward my house, a refurbished family place that sat across a dirt road from the landing and the river. Through the thick growth of trees, I could see a bit of the porch in the twilight. Plato, my swamp hound, appeared from nowhere at my side, jumping to lick my fingers. I scratched his ears, too numbed from the events of the day to find words. We headed toward the house where sensor lights popped on as we approached the screened porch.

Inside, I fed Plato and removed myself to the porch. In normal times, I'd sit out here with Pasquin and talk about the dead person, whether he was murdered or not. We had our inklings of what happened to people, and Pasquin often had the sense of a seer, giving hints that led to real solutions. This time it was different. Jimpson was one of his own, and he wasn't here to speculate with me. I missed his rhythmic rocking on the old porch boards, keeping up his old man drone, scaring the night critters with a loud whoop of a joke. "You're not a funeral planner, old man," I said in a whisper.

Plato went for one short run in the swamp before returning to plop on his pillow in a corner of the living room. Sleep seemed to come easy for him. I wondered if he knew Jimpson. He knew most of the swamp people, even visited them on his secret romps.

I showered and hit the bed, wondering if I'd sleep with all the disturbances bouncing around inside my head. It wasn't happening and when I heard tires coming down the lane, I welcomed the activity.

Vernon was still in his uniform when he entered the living room. Plato looked up, wagged his tail, and flopped back into doggie sleep.

"Thanks, dog, for the welcome," said Vernon. He pulled me close, but I backed away quickly.

"It's the odor," I said. "The faint odor of death."

"Not surprised," he said. "I've got a change of clothes here, right?"

I led him upstairs where he showered and pulled on some pajama bottoms he kept in my house. We had never moved in together, but we were ready for any stay-overs with essentials. I tossed his uniform into the washer.

"Don't put any scented cloth in with it," he said. "Last time, I smelled like old lady lavender all day long."

It was an attempt at humor that didn't work. I joined him on the couch and snuggled into his arms, my face against his bare chest.

"Any word on what's going on?"

"Not with Jimpson, not yet anyway." He stroked my hair, still damp from the shower. "The other matter is bothering us even more."

I lifted my head, "The body you pulled from the bayou?"

"We've been searching the waters for a couple of days, looking for a fisherman that never came home and may have fallen from a boat in the bay. When we didn't find him further out, we followed the current. Found him this morning."

"That would have been search only, right? Then why was Tony and homicide there?"

"They're always called on something like this, when cause of death is unknown. And, right now it looks like homicide instead of drowning. In fact, the body doesn't look like it hit water at all and the currents had nothing to do with where it ended up."

The room grew too silent, and Plato looked up from his pillow as if asking what happened to the people here.

"How?"

"Head trauma." Vernon turned toward me. "That's company secret right now. No telling anyone, including Pasquin."

"Especially Pasquin," I said. "He'll know soon enough. I swear the frogs hop over to his house and tell him the news."

"Be nice if the frogs would tell us who and why, wouldn't it?"

"Then you wouldn't have a job?" I tweaked his cheek and he smiled at me. "It's late."

We headed upstairs to the rhythm of Plato's tail beating against the pillow.

Sleep came easily after a while, and both us drifted into oblivion in each other's arms. Just before my brain shut off, Vernon whispered, "Tony wants you to help look for a weapon in the river. Early start."

Plato made sure we had an early start. He was pushing his paws against my side of the bed about the time the sun appeared through the humid mist. I moaned and trotted downstairs to open the door for him. Behind me, Vernon groaned and pushed himself out of bed.

"That dog is better than an alarm clock," he said. We sat at the kitchen table and ate cereal while Plato gulped down his morning ration of dog food. He'd be out the door and exploring the swamp for hours. I tried not to think of him caught in the vice of gator jaws, but he seemed to know how to avoid that.

"At least we don't have to iron your uniform this morning," I said. "Nice warm day for diving in cold water."

"Grassy water," he smiled. "You're going to love that. Groping around in the stuff for a limb or stick of some kind." He leaned forward, kissed my cheek, and added, "Be sure you don't grab a moccasin instead."

We loaded my diving gear into Vernon's car. His would be at the site in the diving trailer. We bumped along the lane until we came to the paved road and finally the highway. After another narrow paved road and another dirt lane, we pulled in beside the dive trailer at the bridge. Uniformed deputies stood around, watching the area of scene tape still around Jimpson's store. A few people had gathered near the top of the bank to watch, but deputies kept them back far enough to make them uncomfortable in the scrub brush and trees, where they'd have to watch where they stepped in case a rattler was resting in the sun. No one was allowed to stand on the bridge itself. Cars were stopped and allowed to progress only after being warned not to toss anything into the water. Boats were turned back if they were headed out to the bay. This meant they'd have to go back upriver and cross to a water lane into another river altogether for a day's fishing. I could hear them swearing.

There were four of us in dive gear. Vernon and I took the side nearest Jimpson's to search the shallows first. The eel grass grew tall and thick here and waved like snake heads in the currents. With lamps on our masks and gloves on our hands, we sifted through the growth, looking for any form of tool that could be used to bop someone over the head. We found several heavy limbs in various stages of decay and pulled them up to shore where a deputy collected them in a bag. Scene techs in white coats stood back a little, but would look over each specimen to see if it looked like it had been used recently for murder. In a river so close to ancient oaks, this would be a long process.

I had gathered all the limbs I could find in my designated area and motioned to Vernon that I was heading a bit further out from shore. He nodded in the clear water, then pointed at something. A large gray form, rounded and swimming slowly looked at us as we swam toward it. Manatees abounded in these warm waters and none seemed the least perturbed by boats or human divers. This one eased on towards the bay, not darting away in fear, but seeming to snub those of us who had to wear breathing devices to handle the depths.

The grass didn't grow as high in the deeper areas, and the branches were obviously older, but we collected some anyway. Before we were finished with the assigned area, we ran into three more manatees, two large ones and a younger one. The smaller one swam near us for a while, staring, until he got bored and went on to the warm bay.

The other two divers found less than we did, but before we called it quits, we decided to look past the bridge where the river opened into the bay. The tide was beginning to come in and just maybe it would pick up something tossed from the other side and wash it our way.

The tidal waters were against us as we tried to rummage through the grass. The banks near the bridge were lined with river rock and some broken concrete. Single blades of the deep green eel grass grew from narrow cracks. The manatees stayed away from the rock siding, but I was betting it wasn't because they knew it might scratch their skin. They stuck to the deeper channels in the middle of the river lane, at least I thought they did. Vernon and I both caught site of something large snagged on a jutting piece of concrete. I expected to see a dead manatee, its heavy body bloated with gases and decomposing under water.

We moved closer, both of us stopping our swim abruptly and staring at the large piece of gray material clinging to the broken edge. Torn in many places, it was still recognizable as an overcoat of some kind, perhaps a raincoat made of canvas.

I moved closer and grabbed the piece that was waving in the currents while Vernon took the other side. He pulled on an edge of hemmed material. As we pulled back the coat, a belt buckle appeared, then dropped into the flowing water. I made an attempt to grab it, causing me to jerk my end of the cloth. I realized then it was a sleeve, or what was left of one, and it had an arm inside it, or what was left of one.

"Bones in coat," said Marshall Long, who had two of his techs drag the coat to a level place up the bank. "Not all the bones." He looked up at Vernon and me. We had shed our fins and masks but stood near our find. It was a raincoat all right, a cloth one that had been through lots of swift currents. It's wearer had nothing much left except a ragged leather belt and two arm skeletons. I had managed to grab hold of the belt buckle and hand it over to Marshall.

"You're going to have to go back in," he said. "Look for a skull and some more of the body bones. From the looks of this, he's been in the water a while and the bones could be out at sea or at the bottom of the river."

"Or in some sharks belly," said Vernon.

The other two divers grabbed some orange sodas and handed them over to us. We knew the day was going to be a lot longer than expected. Searching for human bones would be difficult at best in these currents after such a long time.

"How do you know it's a he?" I asked Marshall.

"Don't. But, the coat is large, a man's garment I would think. And, the wrists and hands appear larger than a woman's would be. Belt buckle, too, looks like something a man might wear."

"Anything in the pockets?"

"Nothing. It could be a large woman wrapped in a man's coat. Won't know until something tells me more, or you find the rest of this person."

He reached out an arm toward a tech who grabbed hold of it with both hands. It was Marshall's way of balancing himself. He rarely got down on his knees. As he said, that was like moving a mountain to get up again. Instead, he bent his over his heavy belly, nearly standing on his head to look at something on the ground.

"See this." He waved a bulky finger above the area where the left arm would have joined the shoulder, had the shoulder been there. "Bone erosion. Won't know for sure, but I'd say this man got injured sometime in his life."

CHAPTER SIX

The four of us spent another three hours searching the area near the bridge and the side walls. My arms ached from holding myself steady against the incoming tide, trying to focus on the nooks and crannies of both river bottom, stacks of rock, and the forever waving eel grass.

"Nothing, Tony," I said as I joined the others at the surface. We handed off our tanks to waiting deputies. "I'd say if there ever was a skull in this area, it could be near Fogarty Spring by now." I slapped the fins on the bank and raised an arm for help out of the water.

"And," said Vernon who followed me, "the other parts could have been lost at sea." He plopped on the bank and rubbed his face with his hands. "I hope you don't expect us to search this entire river."

The other two divers climbed on shore, one calling for sodas. The other lay back on the dirt, his knees in the air. All of us wanted out of the dive suits.

Tony, always the perfectionist, paced the bank.

"We need to talk to some of the regulars who fish out there, the ones who might be in the path of the currents that reach this river." He pointed to the bay. "I'm talking about bay fishermen as well as those in the Gulf." He stared out to sea for a moment.

"Any one boat, in particular?" asked a deputy, his mouth almost upturned in a sarcastic grin.

"Get me names!" roared Tony, embarrassed by his own suggestion at a monumental task for a local sheriff's office. He stopped, took a breath and turned back to the deputy. "Just ask Fish and Game for a list."

The deputy couldn't resist. He was at least twenty years younger than his boss. "It's Fish and Wildlife now, sir." He didn't stick around for the snarl, but moved the crowd away and pulled out his cell phone.

"We need to talk to the locals, too," said Tony, finally ignoring the upstaging. "What about these fish camps around the bridge area."

"The main one," said Vernon, shading his eyes from the sun, "is at the mainland entrance to the bridge area. Some short timers but several regulars who spend the entire season swatting sand flies."

"And there is Ciel," I said. "The one settled by the storm refugees." I glanced up at Tony. "Near the spot where I saw you earlier today."

Tony paced some more. He worked his jaw and stared at the sky trying to make up his mind about something. I lay back next to Vernon and shaded my own eyes from the sun that was about to disappear behind rain clouds. That's when I felt Tony's feet near me.

"Do you think you could stick around that place?" He said it softly, glancing to his sides to make sure no one heard him. I wasn't a deputy, just an adjunct diver, but he had let me know numerous times that I was an officer of the law anytime I worked for the department.

"Snoop?" I smiled without looking at him.

"Something like that," he said. "Take that old man with you."

"That old man wants to have a river funeral for his friend. Will you allow it?" It was a bit of a bribe, I knew, but if I had to act in a capacity other than my official one, I deserved something. So did Pasquin.

Tony took an audible breath. "He'd do it anyway, wouldn't he? Parade his boats down the river, singing hymns."

"I promise you. He won't sing hymns."

Tony paced. He suddenly turned back and leaned over me. "Do it," he said and walked away.

I looked at Vernon. He smiled a bit but turned serious. "It's not safe."

I sighed. "I'm not teaching summer classes," I said.

"What about the scuba lessons for Sissy?" He referred to a young girl who had been rescued from another case. I'd promised her lessons every Saturday morning.

"She's in diving camp. Iris found one and sent her there. I'll see her again in the fall." Iris Henderson, her guardian, had taken on a child at an advanced age with the gusto of a new mother hen— or maybe grandmother hen. She had retired from teaching linguistics before my time, but we ended up in the same department.

"I know you, Luanne. Remember? You'll do this and Pasquin will chuckle all the way through it."

"I'll be careful, and you'll be around, right?"

He finally relaxed and pushed a smile onto his face. He nodded. "Your knight in shining dive suit."

"It's not like I don't worry, too, you know." I turned my head toward him. The others had drifted off to chat in small circles. "I had a brief moment of terror when I saw a body being hauled out of the woods."

Vernon nodded. Neither of us could think of anything else to say. He would continue to be a deputy and I would snoop. There would be no more argument. The whole process came to a loud halt when thunder rumbled across the sky. It was time to look for shelter.

The rain poured down as we sat in sweltering patrol cars. Tony, always wanting to save money, frowned on keeping the AC running. Too many complaints had been written about government waste in the local paper. I remembered reading about cops sitting in running cars while they ate their hamburgers outside a fast food joint.

"Where did Kayleen get the money to open that café?" said Vernon. He wore only the pants to his uniform at the moment. I wasn't so lucky. I had to pull on a tee shirt with my jeans.

"Saved for it so Mama tells me. I think Bub did a lot of the fix up work."

"She's buying off the boats, then?"

I shrugged. "Seems likely. Fresh seafood and all. They sell close by. Why not?"

"You know anything about the others in that shopping—what would you call it—strip mall?" He laughed. "Stripped down motel would be more like it."

"Just what Pasquin has told me." I turned toward him. "You know you could check into the junk man's background. Harold something. He's got some kind of criminal record according to rumor."

"Let's find some last names, okay?" He paused. "And I want to know who that PI is asking questions about."

"Someone named Janine, hired by the Guerrin family. That's what I overheard." I poked his side. "See. I know how to snoop."

Marshall Long had transported his bodies back to the lab, and the techs cleaned up their tools. It was an exodus out of the swampy bank area of vans and patrol cars, followed by unmarked cars that might as well have insignia on the doors since it was so obvious there were lawmen inside. A lone patrol car would stay behind with a couple of men on guard shift. A patrol boat would make slow passes up and down the river in case another bone washed into view.

Later that night, around closing time, Vernon and I went up the steps of Mama's Place in search of food. My cupboard was bare, as was his.

"You'll have to take leftovers," she said. She had jerked off her apron and sat fanning herself with a menu at the front table.

"We'll take anything," I said. "Can you sit with us for a moment?"

Mama stopped fanning. She glared at me, her tiny eyes in the round face came alert to something shadier than fried fish and grits. She nodded slowly, then yelled for a waiter to bring out what he had in the back.

We took chairs at a table near the kitchen entrance. A few stragglers were eating in the front area near the big window that looked over the river and dock area. The kitchen help had scraped together cheese grits, fried mullet and oysters, along with cole slaw that would have been tossed out because the cabbage would sour before morning.

"Sorry, hush puppy mix was all used up," said Mama. "But some lemon pies are just coming out of the oven." She made them at night and placed them in the refrigerator for the next day's dessert. Most people were used to eating them cold, the lemon tart and firm. But warm from the oven had its own taste, a softer lemon flavor and closer to liquid consistency. It felt like home.

Mama swirled a saucer of grits and ate in small spoonfuls between long swigs of iced tea. "Now, what's the topic?" she whispered.

"I want to know about the people at Ciel," I said. I glanced toward Vernon.

Mama looked at both of us. "You want to know ABOUT them?" she said. "Not just a little sketch, I assume."

"Right," I said.

Vernon said nothing, just raised his eyebrows in agreement.

"I'm going to spend more time around there. Pasquin, too, I hope. Let me know if you have any deliveries you want to make to Kayleen."

Mama kept nodding. Even when she yelled for pie, she was nodding.

It was after midnight when Vernon and I, weary from diving and traveling uneven roads, arrived at my swamp house on the river. No Plato greeted me at the door. I figured he'd given up and gone to Pasquin's for his evening meal. The sensor lights popped on as we approached the screen door to the porch. Inside, the message light was on the answering machine.

"You need to call me when you get in," said Pasquin's gravel voice. "I'll be up late with some people." He didn't use his usual affectionate "ma'am" with me. I knew he was grieving but tears weren't his style.

"Call him," said Vernon, who headed upstairs. "He's up to something."

As soon as he answered, I heard the background chatter and clinking glasses or bottles, depending on what Pasquin's fellow swamp rats were drinking tonight.

"We've got a cremation set up soon as they release the body," he said. "Can you ask your deputy what we need to do about a boat procession and strewing?"

"I've already done that. Tony will okay it. There is another problem, however."

"Yeah. I heard. You got some bones in a coat."

"How in the world!" I knew the swamp vine was good but sometimes it made no sense. The group around the discovery of those bones had been all law enforcement. Yet, someone who lived in that area knew what we'd found.

"Lots of tree houses around there. We old folks know what binoculars are, too," he said. I heard him chuckle for the first time in a while. The tree houses he referred to were small platforms kids had built in oak branches to sit on and sometimes swing from into the swimming areas of the river. Some of them had nails or small boards leading upwards in ladder fashion.

"You don't mean someone was up a tree and watching our every move?" I knew it was useless to wait for an answer. Maybe they were up there. Or in the bushes, on a boat behind a growth of reeds or cypress knees. Spying among the local river inhabitants was an art as ancient as the river itself.

"We plan to release the ashes right at the river mouth, just after the bridge. That's what he wanted." Pasquin turned away from the phone then came back with "men want to know how soon we can expect the body."

"Marshall Long will have to determine that," I said. "I'll ask."

"By the way. Your hound is here. Mourning with the rest of us."

"Mourning? You're not giving him bourbon, I hope."

"Bourbon? A little beer with his bone, maybe."

It wasn't true. I knew Pasquin wouldn't feed a dog beer, but Plato would be basking in the attention he'd get from old men who had seen it all in their swamp, yet managed to change nothing. They'd sit in Pasquin's living room with too much furniture and take turns scratching Plato's wiry hair until the dog would flop beneath the window air conditioner and let the drone lull him into dog sleep. By that time, all the old men would be asleep in their chairs, snoring and making night sounds just like the insect and reptilian world outside the walls.

The rain pounded nearly all night. I lay beside a sleeping Vernon, his slow breathing giving me the comfort that he was here and not in that body bag on the patrol boat. I shivered. Turning towards him and snuggled against the taut skin, I counted my blessings as wind slung the rain against the windows.

I'm not sure when I drifted off, but sun was peeping through the trees on the east side of the house when Vernon's cell phone rang. He moved quickly, trained to be suddenly alert. I rested on my elbows and tried to clear my head. I went downstairs and looked outside at the puddles and the muddy road. Limbs were down in the little bit of yard I had. It had been a hard rain, most likely several inches.

Vernon stood at the top of the stairs. "We need to go," he said. "The patrol boys found something."

A quick shower and orange juice got us out the door. Our diving gear had been left with the team trailer. We were headed for a private home and dock further inland from the bridge but still in the area of swift currents.

The house, a recent construction on stilts belonged to a retired boat salesman from Atlanta. He had used it, he said, for fishing vacations but more often now, he just lived in it since his wife died. He had made coffee and offered us cups as soon as we crossed his dock.

"Long is here," said a deputy. "He came with donuts, but I think he ate all of them."

We walked to the end of the dock, passing a sleek fishing boat named Irma. The man from Atlanta followed us and stood beside Irma as though protecting his property.

"Nothing like a pounding rainstorm to stir up the river," said Marshall Long. His white coat was dotted with colored bits that had topped his donut. "Smiley here looks happy to have been found." He pointed to a skull, its perfect teeth showing a grin from its perch on the edge of the dock atop a black tarp.

"Part of the body in the coat?"

"Ask him," said Marshall, pointing to the white skull. "I won't know until I run the tests and do the matches."

CHAPTER SEVEN

"Suit up," said Tony who joined us on the dock. "If anything else is around here, we need to find it now."

"Why only two of us today?" I asked.

"Off on other cases, mostly warm salty water. You two do your thing in this cold brine."

I smiled, or rather snarled, at Tony as I passed him on the way to the dive trailer. The water here wasn't cold. It mixed with the warm bay waters. Inward a few miles, it was ice water. Tony never swam, even for fun, as far as I could tell. I had a vision in my head of one day bumping him off the dock at Palmetto Springs, perfectly creased pants and all, so he'd know just how cold the water is there.

Vernon and I did what we could in the swift currents, but the heavy rain had stirred up the bottom to nearly no vision at all. And two divers trying to search the depths of a long, deep river was a bit useless anyway.

"Nothing we can do," said Vernon. "Too murky and too big. If there are any other bones down there, you'd better look at low tide during a drought. Or, maybe wait for them to wash up like the skull did."

We rinsed off and took the dock owner's offer to use his bathroom to dress. The man seemed calm but proud to be in on the fun. I saw him touching the fins and tanks before the deputies stowed them in the trailer.

"Normally pretty dull on this river now that I'm alone," he said. "I never saw any of this stuff up close."

"Have you tried the shops at Ciel?" I asked. "Odd sorts live there. You might fight something of interest."

"Ciel?" The man had never heard of the place. I filled him in.

"And a seafood restaurant will open in a couple of weeks."

Vernon gave me a perplexed look as we headed back to his car.

"Just doing a little advertising," I said.

Tony let us know the entire team would meet with Marshall Long in his office tomorrow morning. Marshall would never promise anything so soon, but he'd give what no one would admit would be clever speculation on what he had so far.

"Speaking of Ciel," I said. "What say we head that way after lunch."

"Mama's for lunch?" said Vernon.

The word had been passed around the lunch crowd at Mama's Table that we were looking for bones on the river. It all made one wonder how many old swamp folk were up those trees.

While we waited for a table in the crowded place, Pasquin and two of his friends joined the diners on the steps. The deck at the top was full, and it looked like we might have to hunt up a fast food joint instead.

"Just put us all together," Pasquin yelled at Mama when she stuck her head out the door and yelled for the Comet crew. I took it to mean a bunch of fishermen off a boat named Comet.

We leaned against the gray wood banister and fanned away gnats who were attracted by the humidity and our sweat. In spite of a lot of hand washing and face splashing, the sailors who spent all morning on the river or in the Gulf gave off the distinct odor of salt and fish. Pasquin's buddies, both in work overalls, used the baseball caps they kept in their back pockets to wave in front of their faces. Pasquin made use of his old straw hat as usual. Buzzing mosquitoes never had a chance.

"They need to hurry up," he said. "We're going to be carried off or die from heat out here."

"She got them flowers planted down at the bottom of the stairs," said one man. "Bees'll be flying up here pretty soon."

That started a conversation among several men about how bees were disappearing and honey was going unmade around the area. At least it took some of the discomfort of the dampness away.

Pasquin moved closer to me and held up his hat to cover his mouth. "Look yonder," he said and nodded toward a couple getting out of a car and heading toward the café. "Ain't that your fortune teller?"

A short middle aged woman with white hair had her hand on the arm of a man who looked almost like she did, maybe taller, plumper, and older looking, but similar.

"Sheila, yes," I said. "That's the woman who gives readings in the Talisman.

"Where's the swami hat?" Pasquin said and smiled at his own joke.

"And crystal ball," added Vernon.

The couple joined the crowd on the steps, and I decided if I was going to snoop as Tony put it, this was as good a time as any.

"Hello," I said with a smile and approached Sheila. "Aren't you the reader from the Talisman?"

"Why, yes," Sheila smiled and nodded slowly, a near bow it seemed. "I'm Sheila O'Neil and this is my husband, Fenton."

Fenton stuck out a large hand that gripped mine with strong force. In spite of his age and pudginess, he had strong arms and a grip like steel. He spoke with a deep bass that made me think he could be a singer.

"Nice to meet you," he said.

"You're not from here." I kept smiling while I talked. "I can tell by the accent. New York, maybe?"

"Upstate," he said. "We get down here most summers. I like the fish camp. Sheila here reads and does her card stuff."

"You've given readings other places?" I glimpsed Vernon's sly smile as he stared at the sky.

"Privately," said Sheila. "Until I met Marci Doucet. She has such a lovely shop."

"Yes, I was there earlier and saw you with a customer who seemed a bit upset about a reading."

Sheila frowned for a moment. Her husband put an arm around her shoulder. "Sometimes I don't see good things in cards," she said. "It happens a couple times a week."

I wondered what an odds maker would think of that. Wouldn't it be logical for bad news to occur at least that often when using Tarot cards?

"She actually came out and bought an amulet. Something about water protection," I said. My playacting was beginning to annoy me as well as amuse Vernon.

"Oh! That's Mrs. Cardel. Her husband works on the shrimp boats, and she's always so worried about him." Sheila moved close to me and lowered her voice. "I saw a little trouble for him this time."

"I see. And were you right?"

"Oh, not me, dear. The cards. They're never wrong. But I don't know the details yet. You see, he hires out for long periods on those boats. He's been out at sea for days now. Mrs. Cardel won't know until someone contacts her. If anything is wrong, that is."

"And you said it's for sure, or at least the cards did?"

"Mmmm," she said and gave one brief nod to let me know she wasn't going to give out anything else.

"I saw you earlier in the trailer camp," I said. "You waved as I walked by, not waved exactly, but you gave a funny little gesture that looked like a wave."

Sheila giggled and dimpled up her sweating face. "It's just a little piece of magic I cooked up myself. Kind of like a gesture of protection."

I smiled and nodded, not seeing how a two-finger motion could protect me from anything.

"I'll try to come by for a reading myself one day soon," I said, biting my tongue for not knowing who was the bigger charlatan, me or Sheila.

Mama appeared in the doorway and hollered "Pasquin! Table for five."

Inside, the air conditioning struggled to eliminate the humidity from outside and rising off hot bodies, but it was losing. Huge platters of fried fish added to the heat.

"Wouldn't it be better to serve cold salads instead," I said as we pulled chairs close the table and close to each other.

"Don't get sacrilegious, woman," said Pasquin. "We don't come here for cold salads. Only cold stuff we want is a jar of iced tea."

"You'll get a big glass like everybody else, old man," said Mama. "Now what does everybody want?" She swiped a napkin across her forehead as each person ordered. She never wrote it down, but said she remembered all of it. What difference did it make if you got grouper instead of mullet?

The O'Neils came in and sat at a table for two near a window. While Pasquin traded river stories of the day with Vernon and his two friends, I watched the elderly couple. They studied a menu and waited for someone to take the order. Sheila put one hand to her forehead and rubbed it like someone with a headache—or maybe a vision of crisis. Her husband stretched his solid arm and patted hers. Sheila then placed a finger from each hand at her temples and massaged them. As the fingers moved closer to her white hair, something didn't seem right. The movement was off, like something going against the current.

"My oh my! It's a wig," I said under my breath.

"What is?" Vernon had been watching me the entire time I was watching the O'Neils.

"Sheila the reader. She's got on a wig."

Vernon half laughed. "Suits her. At least it's not some long black witch's locks."

Sheila put her hands down and smiled up at the waitress while her husband ordered. Despite his pudginess, he ate his seafood platter down to the flounder backbone. Sheila picked at hers, finally shoving aside the plate with untouched fish filets.

"You got your holy shrimp on?" said Pasquin, his voice breaking into my speculation on what Sheila might look like without the rug.

"Oh, yeah," I pulled the talisman on a chain from my purse. "It doesn't work with a dive suit." I thrust it over my head and tucked it beneath the tee shirt. "Wouldn't look too good with cheese grits, either."

Pasquin chuckled and began relating the Talisman's shop contents to his friends. They laughed with him and began telling stories of charms and ghosts their grandpas had heard in their days.

"One old fellow done got him a pointed rock from down by Palmetto Springs. Said it was given him by an old Indian and it might save him from snake bite. Did, too." He laughed and stuffed fish into his mouth. "That pointed rock was most likely an arrowhead, and he used it to draw poison."

"That ain't the story you told me," said the other man who was using his fingers to pull flesh off the fish backbone. "You said he used it to deliver a baby out in the swamps, cut the cord and all."

"That, too," he said. "And that baby grew up to know how to talk to animals in the woods. People said he could walk around in pitch black night and wouldn't a snake come near him. Not even a gator."

I looked at Pasquin and smiled. "I guess that baby was you."

They all laughed with me, except Vernon. His attention was at the front door. Tony had entered and was scanning the room. He joined us, but looked annoyed when he saw Pasquin and friends who had no intention of giving up the table.

"I need to see you outside," he said to Vernon. "Keep his food warm, okay?" He nodded toward me.

Without thinking, I pulled at the chain around my neck and began rubbing the holy shrimp. After some moments, Vernon waved me to the door.

"They identified the body we pulled from the bayou," he said in a low voice. "Husband of a woman who lives near the fish camp."

Mama saw us standing there and held up a doggie bag from across the room. Vernon nodded. She headed for our table to pack up the rest of our food.

CHAPTER EIGHT

"We identified his fingerprints," said Tony as we made our way to the cars. "He's a fisherman on the shrimp boats."

"Seasonal hired help?" asked Vernon.

Tony nodded. "Lives in a little old wood frame house down from the fish camp."

"Ciel," I said. "He has a name?"

"Ben Cardel," he said. "You know him?"

We didn't know him but we had seen his wife before we ran into her at the crime lab ID morgue. The limp hair and knotty joints were a clue, but the amulet around her neck pinpointed her identity. We waited while she went in with a friend, as skinny and as defeated as the wife, to look at the man on the guerney behind the glass. A single hoarse scream let us know she recognized him. We stood away from the door as she gripped the arm of her friend and muttered down the hall, "I knew something was wrong. Sheila was right. Something was wrong. He was away too long." She shook her head, not so much in denial as in dismay, as a deputy led her to an interview room.

"That's Belinda Cardel," said Tony. "Wife of the fisherman. She's crying now, but I wonder for how long. The man got nasty when he was home and had too much to drink."

"You mean he didn't just jab at demons like Gibby in the trailer-park?"

"Jabbed at her in their little house," he said. "Don't know how they could stand living in that tiny place."

"Might have been okay when he was away," I said, privately blanching at the thought of some man coming home with a small check, too much rum, and a fierce temper.

"Who is the woman with her?" asked Vernon.

Tony shrugged. "I'm assuming a neighbor, but maybe a relative. We don't ask. Just glad they are doing the supporting and we don't have to."

He headed to the interview room, but motioned us on past toward Marshall Long's office. "He'll brief you on what he knows so far, with his usual disclaimer, of course."

The familiar sight of Marshall's office was never comforting. All the instruments of gouging and poking dead men were visible through a second door, away from his swivel chair and microscope. Files and papers littered the utility desk like too many bodies in a storm, waiting to be buried.

"Drag 'em up," he said, keeping his eye on the scope and waving his arm about the room.

"Okay if we move some stuff?" I said.

Marshall grunted, and Vernon gently put down more stacks of paper on the floor near the other two chairs on rollers in the room. As soon as we were seated, he swung his huge body around with the agility of a skate board. I had the feeling of a large boulder about to land in my lap.

"Sorry. Did I scare you?" He grabbed a large soda cup and sucked on the straw until it rattled. "How come you didn't bring drinks?"

"I'll be happy to fill your cup at the fountain," I said.

"Water? Never!"

He tossed the cup into an overflowing trash bin and leaned

forward. It appeared he was rubbing his legs near the knees. "Been sitting too long in one position." He grabbed hold of the edge of the desk and stood up, making more grunting sounds. "Let's walk."

Instead of strolling the long hallway, he turned back into the examining room behind his own office. The coat from the arm bones we had found near the bridge lay on a metal table.

"This thing has no label," he said. "The material seems to be foreign, but we have to check that out with some textile experts. One thing for sure is that the size was too big for the arms. Given the measurements, a live person with those arms in these sleeves would not show any hands. Now, I don't know for sure anything, okay? But, the hands and wrists seem thick but small, maybe a woman's. Fully grown, so we're not talking a child and no sign of dwarfism or deformities. The big coat may be a man's given the side the buttons are on and the way it covered the arms." He never touched the coat but ran his heavy fingers over the air above the area of discussion.

"There are some belt loops as well as that man's belt we found with the coat. No coat belt, however. It might have come loose or never used. That buckle you found could have been part of another belt used to bind the body in the coat." Marshall stood over the coat and made a tying motion with his hands. "I'm guessing, but I'd say the arms were in the sleeves and the sleeves pulled together and tied with something. That's why the hand bones stayed with the arm bones. I figure there was more skeleton but it pulled loose and floated out to sea through the neck and bottom areas. We got arms because they stayed in a tied up bundle."

"A female who has been wrapped in a man's raincoat and tossed into the ocean," I said. "Anyone looking for a wife missing around here?"

"Ask Tony. Not my job." Marshall grabbed an enlarged photograph of the hand bones. "And I'm not saying it is a woman. Look at the finger bones. I'd say this person had stubby little hands, ones that would make nice fists or nail boards together."

"Now," said Vernon, "you are guessing and not based on much."

Marshall smiled. "What they aren't are slender fingers of an artist." He held up his hand in protest. "I know, I know. I'm way off base. Just like to speculate, be a little subjective at times."

"Before you tell us she was not a ballet dancer, did you find any flesh or bits of other clothing?" I shrugged my shoulders in his direction.

"Ooh, you've been watching the shows," he said. "Nope. Nothing. I'll speculate further that the bones were put into the coat and tossed. Flesh was rotting off or already gone." He lifted his eyes with a nod. "Little fish or crabs got the rest."

The three of us stood silently staring at the coat with sleeves that had kept hold of arm and hand bones but nothing else.

"Any chance that only the arms and hands were wrapped in the coat?" said Vernon, breaking the silence and causing me to jump.

"Could be, but why use the whole coat?" Marshall went silent again.

"We're looking at a situation where someone kept a skeleton somewhere until all the flesh was gone," I said, the goose bumps rising on my own arms. "Then he took her to sea and dumped her."

"And her skull came off and we found it farther up river?" said Vernon.

Marshall shifted his weight and frowned. "Doubt that scenario. The skull was male."

"It's not unusual to find bones in a river that came in on ocean tides," I said. "Could be a drowning victim. The skull, I mean. This poor lady's bones were wrapped and tossed."

"Either way, Tony has to look at it as a homicide," said Vernon.

Tony was still inside the interview room with Mrs. Cardel when we left the building. Outside, dark clouds gathered and lightning flashed in the distance.

"We need to figure out how to be in Ciel more often," I said. "At least I do. You can wear the uniform and claim jurisdiction."

"I've been talking to your old friend," said Vernon. "Pasquin suggested you borrow a trailer and hook up there." He turned his face as if to look at the coming storm and laughed. "I can see you now in an old silver Airstream, trying to turn around and put on a dive suit."

"I'm not staying down there," I said. "But I don't think it's a bad idea for the department to set up something like that." I smiled back at him. "Like a small trailer for one—maybe two—people and a place for a red canoe on the side."

He was giving me an evil eye when drops of rain began to pelt the hot parking lot surface. We headed back inside.

We waited in the lobby while sheets of rain blocked all view of the cars. Tony finally emerged from an elevator with another deputy, telling him to drive the two ladies home.

"She's shook up, but she'll survive it," he said. "But she won't get the body anytime soon for a funeral." He turned around to see the second elevator door open and a technician escorting Mrs. Cardel and her friend to the lobby. "We'll take care of them from here on," he said to the technician.

The deputy guided the two ladies to the end of the hall where there was a shelter to avoid rain. It was actually the place where they took bodies in and out of coroner's wagons and hearses, but in a storm, the ladies wouldn't know that.

"She say anything?" asked Vernon.

Tony gave me the suspicious eye, a habit of his, until he reminded himself I would be a part of the dive effort. He motioned for us to follow him away from the two elevators.

"She said he left three weeks ago to work on a shrimp boat in the Gulf. Should have been home four days ago. Sometimes they stay out longer, or he gets a small job like filling in for a sick sailor while he's out there, so she didn't get too disturbed that he wasn't home on time." He took a deep breath. "Now, get this. She'd cleaned the house and had his favorite roast cooked for him the day he was due back. I got this feeling that's why she was worried. Like he was going to be all upset that the food was old or not edible by the time he got there, and his temper would flare. She wasn't worried he'd drowned or anything like that, just that the meal she fixed wasn't going to be good enough for him when he did finally return."

"Not something she needs to worry about now, is it?" I said.

"Any word on the autopsy results?" asked Vernon.

"Not yet. He had head trauma as you know, and some bruises, but we won't know for a couple of days."

The rain let up enough for all of us to make it back to the cars. Thunder sounded in the distance, indicating the storm was passing fast to the east.

Vernon drove until we were well out of the rain and the sun baked down on humid air that felt like a steam bath. No one drove with the windows down, but blasted the air conditioners as hard as their engines would allow. Puddles of water stood in the middle of the paved roads and washed out holes in the dirt ones. It would have been one of those rainstorms that produced three inches of rain in a matter of minutes.

We left our muddy shoes on the porch and walked barefoot across the boards into the house. Rain had blown through the screens and the rocking chairs were wet. It was too humid to sit outside anyway, and I let them dry naturally.

"Plato found shelter, I guess," said Vernon.

"Most likely at Pasquin's," I said and flipped on the ceiling fan. It was supposed to blow the cool air from the conditioner and save money on electricity. I wondered if it didn't just blow river dust up our noses.

I poured sodas over ice and we sat in the living room, not moving so as to not stir up heat.

"We've got maybe three bodies out of the water," said Vernon.

"And another on land," I said, remembering Jimpson and the sadness of his funeral that would happen soon.

In the distance, we heard a bark and finally heavy steps on the porch. Pasquin had arrived with Plato.

"You got something to wipe the mud?" he called from the door.

I dragged a ragged towel to the porch and wiped Plato down until he only smelled like wet dog but wouldn't track mud inside. Pasquin pulled off his boots.

We sat at the kitchen table and listed to Plato slobber through a meal of dog food and water. He huddled for moment near me for an ear scratch but decided flopping beneath an air conditioning vent was better.

"You know anyone with a trailer we can borrow?" asked Vernon.

"Borrow? Sheriff's office must have plenty of trailers."

"Not a marked one. Something a vacationer with not too much money might park at Ciel for a week or so." Vernon smiled at Pasquin.

Pasquin winked and nodded. "Must be one somewhere. Guess you're wanting it big enough for you and the lady, here."

"No bigger than that," said Vernon.

CHAPTER NINE

Pasquin delivered. One of his deep swamp friends had a camper trailer he'd just cleaned out after a trip half way down the state. We could borrow it as long as we wanted, and he would register it with the park in his name.

"It's not exactly one of those classy Airstreams," I said as I watched Vernon and the owner pull it into a space near the old dock, the last one on the edge of Ciel.

"It's got the hook up stuff. Good stove, places for two to sleep," Pasquin turned to me and winked. "Of course, can't but one person sleep to a bed."

I rolled my eyes at him and changed the subject. If I let him, he'd be into making jokes about a bouncing trailer. Vernon positioned the small, rectangular abode atop the markers and proceeded to hook up water, electricity, and sewage. We had the space indefinitely because the sheriff had arranged it with the owner of the camp, but we were telling everyone it would probably be for a two week canoeing vacation. I had my nice red canoe on top of my car, ready to be unloaded and secured next to the trailer.

"It's not much of a pretty thing," said Vernon as he stepped back and eyed the squatty trailer. The owner had attempted to remove rust in places, making it look as though the paint had come off over time. A low-hanging oak branch gently scraped the top of the trailer, providing shade, but not cooling. That would have to be from the tiny and aging window air conditioner. It would either be enough to feel like a fan or a meat locker. For certain it would be noisy.

"We better find out something around here," I said. "This is not the Ritz."

"I'll row in my own canoe this afternoon," said Vernon. "Let's move you in." He picked up a duffle bag and a bag of groceries I had sitting on the hood of my little car. We decided to leave the dive gear with the sheriff's dive trailer. It would call too much attention to us.

"Now, people here may know you," Tony had said. "It's okay, but don't let them think you're getting to know them. If they ask, you can tell them you need to be near when we call for another dive. Otherwise, you're just having fun in your canoe."

I figured someone like Kayleen would know enough to find that strange. After all, I lived right in front of the river and a nice landing dock. She didn't comment, however, just seemed happy to have someone around who might help her make decisions at the new café.

"As long as you don't ask me to cook, clean, or wait tables," I said.

My first afternoon at Ciel, I took a lawn chair and sat outside the trailer, batting at gnats and fanning sweat beads. Pasquin sat with me until he couldn't stand it anymore.

"People call this a vacation," he said. "Maybe so, if you like to sit and fish. But, sitting and staring? And what I'm seeing ain't all that pretty."

We were in direct line with the Gibson trailer, but it wasn't entirely visible. Past the clearing, it sat among a heavy growth of pines. A couple of yellow inner tubes lay at the bottom of their three-step entrance.

"You think Gibby gets drunk and rides the river on one of those?"

"Wouldn't think so. He'd drown in the currents."

Tubing was a considered a sport on some rivers in the state, but it wasn't all that popular around here. Occasionally, you'd see a group of teens trying it out and flowing with the currents, but not adults. It required too much agility for most of them.

Carol Gibson emerged from her trailer. She held a hand painted sign that said FOR RENT $5/HALF DAY, and leaned it against the tubes.

"Extra money," said Pasquin. "Got to keep the old man in his grog."

"Maybe it's to save up for rehab," I added, knowing this would never happen. Gibby would fight those demons as long as he could swing his arms in the air. After that, he'd fight them in his dreams.

"You find them bodies in the water," said Pasquin, his eyes looking philosophical. "What's it like coming across one?"

"It's different for me in a dive suit. I'm looking for one or at least a sign of one. Gibby was about to become one in that Orleans flooding. If a dead body came at him in rushing, filthy water, he'd see himself in the next hour or so, floating by in the same condition." I looked at Pasquin.

"Wonder if he was full of liquor when he was being washed away?"

"Somehow, old man, I think a lot of them were. You're in a bar, didn't find safety out of the area or in a shelter like you were told. Instead, you try and drink your way through it in a local bar. Next thing you know, you and your buddies and the bottles are headed down the street on a wave of water. Must have beat the macho right out of those fellows."

Pasquin chuckled and shut his eyes. "Another one of your male things," he said as he drifted into a doze.

I closed my eyes, too, letting the gnats swirl around me all they wanted. The heat and the river made lethargy set in, and I was nearly asleep when a male voice above me said, "Is that canoe yours?"

I jumped. My head, tilted back in the chair, looked up at a heavy man with lots of eyebrows. It would have been a kind face had it not been for the cold stare of his gray eyes.

"Mr. O'Neil," I said and raised to an upright sitting position. I glanced at Pasquin who opened one eye just a slit, then closed it again. "Yes, I own the canoe. I'm hoping to have some fun rowing it on the currents."

"Isn't it dangerous out here in this part of the river?"

I looked around at the red canoe, its name, Peace Offering, painted on the side. "Not if you know what you're doing, and you can swim. I've got both talents," I said and smiled back at him.

"My wife likes to go boating," he said it to the air, like he was thinking out loud. "But she's too old to do it now."

"Does she like to ride in a boat with someone else doing the rowing?"

He shook his head, looking at the trees around him. He glanced at me and said, "We had some appointments up in Tallahassee this morning. Riding anything tires her out. She's resting now."

"No readings today?"

"She doesn't make appointments for readings when she has other things pressing."

"How long has she done that sort of thing, like Tarot cards and such?"

"Long time. She's really good at it. You'd be surprised."

"She seemed to get Mrs. Cardel right," I said. "Even if it was negative."

He shrugged like someone on a New York street would have done. "Lots of negativity in this world. She reads. Doesn't control."

Pasquin stirred and said, "Might be nice if someone could. Might not get so many dead bodies around here."

I changed the subject. "Do you think Sheila would do an abbreviated reading, maybe a palm reading, for me?"

Mr. O'Neil stared at both of us for a moment. He nodded and waved quickly, and without another word, strolled away.

"Man is out of place down here," said Pasquin.

I turned to him when O'Neil had passed from my vision into the trees. "Most New Yorkers I know, the ones who come down here, do it in the winter time. He says they come every year. It's summer. Do they like this heat and the bugs?"

"Must do. Or he ain't telling the truth," said Pasquin. "Fancy that."

"I'll offer his wife a ride in the canoe one day. Maybe she can see the future in an eddy somewhere."

"Better give her a life jacket," said Pasquin as he turned his head and closed his eyes.

It wasn't something I was used to doing, but I figured I'd need jackets for anyone getting into the canoe with me. I pulled the cell phone from my pocket and called Vernon.

The day lazed on, and our conversation turned into naps interrupted by horse flies and the occasional breeze. At one point, I thought I heard a boat motor go by, but maybe I dreamed it. The small boats with one or two fishermen hadn't come in from the Gulf yet, and it was too soon for any shrimpers to arrive with a catch.

The next time I awoke, it was to the slamming of a truck door and loud shouts.

"Sounds like Bub and Kayleen done had a disagreement," said Pasquin. He grunted and shoved himself to a half standing position. "And I've got to move or these old joints will freeze up on me." He pushed upright and strolled toward the clearing. "Yep, it's Bub's truck. He and Kayleen are headed for their trailer."

"It won't be their last disagreement," I said. "Owning and running a restaurant is not an easy job, and it's nonstop."

"Another van coming in behind his truck." Pasquin shaded his eyes with his hand and watched two men knock on the trailer door. "Can't see what's written on the van."

I leaned forward and squinted. "Sign painters," I said. "Bet they're fussing over the name, maybe even the color and the price of having it done."

Pasquin nodded and fanned himself with his hat.

We settled back in our chairs and caught glimpses of two men in white overalls pulling paint cans and ladders from the van. One took a piece of paper to Kayleen, and while they discussed it, Bub jumped into his truck and slammed the door. He had to maneuver between some trees in order to turn around and avoid the paint truck, but he eventually revved the engine and took off, gravel and other debris spraying behind him.

I turned to Pasquin. "Nice being single, isn't it?"

He nodded, then leaned over to slap at me with his hat.

The slow process of the painters put us both to sleep for a short time. I awoke to Pasquin's snore, his chin drooped onto his chest. Replacing his fallen hat on his head, I moved closer to the Romaine's trailer. The painters were lifting a sign to the roof and attaching it to a structure they had put up behind the trailer. It was large, probably too large for the trailer roof to support, thus the structure behind it. Once it was secure, one painter passed paint to another and he busied himself doing a touch up:

Kayleen's Café   Open Everyday 7 am-10 pm   Seafood All Styles.

"So that's what she's going to call the place," I said. "And I'll bet putting the ad sign on the trailer is why Bub got angry."

"You talking to yourself?" Pasquin said in a sleepy tone from behind me.

"Out loud," I said. "Let's go see what she's done to the café itself."

We watched one of the sign painters readjust a sensor light to shine onto the sign. I figured he had fixed it so it would stay on all night and wondered how the neighbors were going to like that.

When the paint truck pulled out, we were right behind it. They turned toward the main road north near the shops, and we parked in front of the café with its new paint on the front wall. Kayleen's Café had been emblazoned across the wall, dark blue and white lettering on a background of aqua waves. Up close, you could catch a pink crab, shrimp or fish darting about the waves. Seafood in its live glory, before being fried or broiled or blackened and served up to hungry fishermen or fortune tellers.

"She got it done," said Pasquin as though he hadn't been sure Kayleen really had it in her. "Guess we better come to the grand opening." He held up a flyer that came from a group stuffed into a box resting at the door.

"She's starting with lunch this Saturday," I said, reading over the flyer with a menu on the back. The printing job was professional. "Looks like she's put some money into this."

We both looked up to see Carol Gibson pull into the parking area. Kayleen came out of the passenger side.

"Are those my flyers?"

I held up the one I was holding. "Nice job."

"I want to pass them around to the boats that come in and to the trailer camp people." She looked at me. "If you're going to Mama's Place, could you give her a handful? She said she'd have one of her helpers pass them out in Fogarty Spring."

I laughed. "Aren't you the competition?"

She smiled. "Not really. At least I don't think Mama looks at it that way."

"Only competition is that old man of hers." Carol Gibson jabbed her thumb toward Kayleen, her face scowling. "But then, that's what old men are good for." She grabbed a flyer and began perusing it.

"She's talking about Bub," said Kayleen. "He's kind of mad about the flyers and the painters. Says I'm putting in too much money." She shrugged.

"And the sign on the trailer top?"

"Oh, dear, yes," she said. "He's not happy about that."

"Downright pissed," said Carol. "It's just all about them, isn't it? Whatever they feel has to be catered to no matter what it does to anyone else." She looked into the trees and went quiet.

Kayleen nodded for us to go inside the café.

"She had another episode with Gibby last night," she said in a low voice, watching to make sure Carol hadn't followed us inside. "She kept him inside, but he ranted at his demons for quite a while."

"Where did he get the liquor?"

"He said someone gave it to him—a woman."

"Carol must have loved that."

"She kind of made a comment about her. I don't think she knows who the woman is, but heaven help her if Carol finds out."

"She'd get violent?"

"Oh, yes. Gibby isn't the only one boxing at evil in that family."

CHAPTER TEN

I sat at a table and sipped tea with Pasquin while Kayleen dealt with delivery men. Her kitchen was spotless. The espresso machine, second hand, sat polished and ready to make the strong brew many of the fishermen from the other side of the Gulf would love.

"You've hired some help, I hope," I asked once when she took a break.

"Carol is going to waitress. I've got a young man coming in to help in the kitchen. But, it's mostly me and the cooking." She looked at me with embarrassed eyes. "Bub is supposed to help, too."

"He will come through, won't he?"

She sighed. "I sure hope so."

Pasquin wandered among the tables. He stopped a few times to stare out the big picture window at Carol who was still resting against her truck. Kayleen had taken her a glass of tea, which had to be warm by now, but she sipped at it anyway. Pasquin just shook his head and moved back to me.

"That woman won't be any use to nobody if she keeps up that brooding. Might just slap a customer up side the head if she thinks he's being sassy."

I stared out at the moody Carol and wondered about her as an employee who had to deal with a husband about to tumble off the edge. Would he stagger into the café one night and fight demons for the customers?

Before I could dream up an image of this destruction, a man appeared at the doorway. I hadn't heard a car drive up, so he must have walked from the other end of the shops.

"Afternoon," he said to Pasquin and me as he swiped his sweaty forehead. He even used the handkerchief like the brim of a hat and kind of tipped it toward us. He leaned his stocky arms on the edge of table as though balancing himself after a hard walk. He wore heavy, clunky shoes that I've often seen short men wear, and wondered if they felt more grounded in them, like they might blow away in a strong wind without the weights.

"I've seen the two of you around these parts and wondered if you would mind helping me with some information." He flipped open his identification. I took it and read it carefully, knowing this wasn't what most people did.

"Mr. Zeke Owen?" I turned to him, and he nodded, looking puzzled. "You're a licensed private investigator." I said it out loud for Pasquin's benefit.

Owen nodded. "Mind if I grab a chair?" He didn't wait for an answer but slid into the chair that faced the door. It was an old habit of careful people, especially cops, to always face the door.

"I'm looking for a missing person."

"Missing from where?" asked Pasquin. He knew, but he would make the man earn his fee.

"Louisiana. She disappeared after the hurricane. Her family figures she went to a shelter and then set up shop or began working somewhere else."

"Why wouldn't she contact them?" I asked.

"Not close." He shook his head and wiped his face again.

"You think she came here?" Pasquin winked at me.

"Could have. She worked with Marci Doucet, the owner of the Talisman. I saw both of you in it the other day."

I pulled the holy shrimp from inside my shirt and waved it in front of his eyes. "Lady said it was empowered by a priestess."

Owen stared at the necklace and nodded a few times. "That priestess could have been Janine Guerrin," he said and pulled a photo from his shirt pocket. "Ever see her?"

Pasquin took the picture and placed it on the table top. We both bent over it. It had to be a publicity photo, posed. The woman wasn't smiling but looked mysterious. She appeared to be a creole with a dark bandana on her head. Multi-beaded earrings hung to her shoulders. The shadowing gave her the quality of someone who used crystal balls.

"Beautiful," I said. "Seems around thirty or forty years old. Knows how to strike a pose."

"Yes, she owned a store like the Talisman but never went back to even see if there was anything salvageable."

"How do you know that?" asked Pasquin. Owen stared at him. "I mean, how do you know she never went back? Were you or her family watching that shop right after the storm left? Now, she could have seen the devastation and said forget it all. Might be in Texas for all you know."

"I've checked Texas shelters. In fact, I've checked all the known shelters. But people took off in all directions. It's hard to track a lot of them. I've been looking for Miz Doucet for quite a while now. Her name finally came up on a business license here in Florida."

"Do you need more tea here?" asked Kayleen as she approached the table. "We aren't open for business yet."

"But I'm on business," said Owen and slapped open his ID again. "Have you seen her?" Again the photo of Janine Guerrin appeared.

"Is she some kind of criminal?" asked Kayleen, barely glimpsing the photo.

"Just a missing person," Owen said and withdrew the picture to his shirt pocket. "I wouldn't mind some tea, and I'll pay for it."

Kayleen waved her hand to refuse money and retrieved the plastic pitcher and a clean glass from the counter.

He took long gulps of the cold tea and let Kayleen refill the glass. He was telling her what he knew about the shop in New Orleans before Katrina when Vernon joined us. Vernon in full deputy uniform.

Owen was facing the door and saw him enter. His voice slowed and he paled for a second. He nearly paralyzed himself as Vernon made straight for our table.

"I thought you might be here," he said to me.

Owen melted a bit, the color returning to his face. He gulped down more tea. Vernon pulled a chair from another table and sat close to me.

"I brought some stuff for you, including life jackets."

I turned and deliberately introduced Owen, who forgot to flash the ID this time. Vernon asked to see it.

"Okay," he said. "Mr. Zeke Owen, licensed PI. What are you doing here?"

The comedy in all this was that we knew already why he was there, and we were just having fun making him repeat it for every person who came in contact with that ID card.

"You want me to run the name through our system?" Vernon asked. "Might tell us if she's in Florida. Might not."

Zeke Owen's big hand shook now as he nodded and smiled at Vernon. "I'd appreciate that. I'm staying here." He pulled out a card, one of probably many he had snitched off his motel's registration counter. It had the manager's name on the front. On the back, he jotted down his name and room number. "Call me." He stopped. "Or I can come in if you like."

"No. I'll call you," said Vernon. He pocketed the card.

"Just be sure if you have to do anything that involves a gun or something else that might be iffy, call us," he said and whipped out his own card.

Zeke Owen nodded and stood up, saying he still had some interviews at the shops. His clunky shoes moved rapidly to the front door where he turned slightly to see all of us staring at him. He waved.

"A PI without a cell phone," said Vernon. "Interesting."

"You needing any décor for that vacation home you got?" Pasquin emptied his tea glass. "I hear that junk man's got some rare stuff."

We walked the few steps across a parking area and stood in front of Harold's Oddities. From outside, it didn't look all that odd. Second hand and junk shops existed up and down the highway leading from the coast inland, and this one had the goods displayed outside just like they did. Of course, this one had Harold displayed, too. Amid iron and brass planters, table frames, and some items that may have been tools though for what I couldn't tell, sat a man with his head tilted back far enough to make his neck hurt when he straightened it. He was in a chair frame that had two pillows on the seat and one behind the man's back— bed pillows. The graying hair and face stubble made him seem old, but the toothless mouth confirmed it. The toothless condition was apparent to the world because he was sound asleep with his mouth open.

"Man is going to feast off gnats if he keeps that up," laughed

Pasquin.

"Should I wake him?"

Before Pasquin could answer, Harold jumped and eyed us while he rubbed his neck.

"Just go on in," he said in a lilt that combined a bit of Cajun with good ol' boy Southern. "You looking for anything special?"

"Browsing," I said.

Pasquin nodded for me to go on inside. He moved closer to the man and introduced himself. There seemed a kind of melding of their voices, the tone and rhythms of two old men who had spent much of their life in Southern swamps. I heard Harold pull up a chair for Pasquin.

Harold's Oddities was more like a dangerous trek for some clumsy person. Iron and old wood stuck out everywhere, like a fungus growing from the walls and floors into the room. I had the feeling that if I touched anything, it would fall and pierce my skin, causing tetanus. Tucked into a corner near the front was an old counter with a stool and something that looked like a receipt book and a pen on top. I suspected that if there was a cash box it was behind the counter on a shelf. Harold didn't seem to worry about it. I took a quick peek and saw nothing but an old phone book. He was probably one of those old time vendors who carried all the cash in his pocket. He'd give a written receipt only if the customer asked for one.

I tried to rummage without upsetting anything, but it was mostly dodging rusty protrusions. On the back wall, I ran into a find, something I hadn't seen since childhood on some farms. A mule harness and yoke rested there, and nearby, an old plow made of steel and two wooden handles. Looking further, I found other remnants of local history, including a peanut boiling barrel. Harold had made his rounds.

"Harold has a boat," said Pasquin when I rejoined them outside the shop. "Goes up and down this river and the others, including our Palmetto."

"Nice rivers," said Harold. He stared up at me with clear eyes. I had figured him for a drunk, but there was no sign of heavy drinking right now.

"He certainly has farm equipment inside," I said. "Do you know that some of that stuff is museum quality, valuable to collectors?"

Harold stared for a moment, then smiled at me. "Farmers wanted it off their hands and out of their barns," he said. "Now, you know some of them museums, just send them here." He nodded after saying that, like affirming his own words.

I promised to do that and bought a hurricane lantern from him. It was rusted but would be a good candle holder for power outages. As I thought, Harold tucked the two dollars I gave him into his money clip and shoved it into his pants pocket.

"You go ahead and visit the Talisman," said Pasquin. "I'll stay here and talk a bit. Here, let me hold onto that for you." He took the lantern.

I walked away from Harold's Oddities, hearing him offer Pasquin a sody-pop, and went to the door with the sprite and her bells.

Marci Doucet was in her blue period today—blue as in color, never in sadness. The scarf material of her top draped over her pale skin and ended in sharp hem angles at her waist. Below that, it was a pair of jeans. She wore a silver necklace with both a cross and a crystal around her neck that ended up in her cleavage. The scarf didn't leave much of her chest to imagination.

"Greetings," she smiled. "You're back. I always know when customers will return."

"How do you know that?" I picked up a bottle of oil marked *tester* and sniffed it.

"You seemed fascinated by the things I have here, and your friend bought you a talisman."

"Yes," I said and touched the chain around my neck.

"Why not wear it outside and let the world see your protection?"

And give you free advertising, I thought. "I guess it's best against the heart," I said and swallowed my urge to be rational.

"You must believe in it since you wear it. It's good to actually believe in these things." Marci's smug smile made me think of yellow canary feathers poking out of the cat's mouth.

"I guess I believe in my friend."

I pretended to try more of the oily perfume testers, even rubbing one on my wrist and dabbing it behind my neck.

"Your friend from the sheriff's department was in earlier." The canary feathers really showed this time.

"Oh?" I hoped she didn't realize my system stopped cold. I had no idea Vernon had been here.

"He asked about Sheila."

I looked toward the back. The door to Readings by Sheila was closed. "He didn't really ask for a reading, did he?"

"I could never reveal that about customers," she said. "Besides, I never know if they make appointments with her or not. But, she's not here today. Feeling a bit unwell, I heard."

"Wouldn't she know something was coming on, being a fortune teller and all?"

Marci gave a small chuckle. "Maybe she did. She didn't tell me."

I moved away from the woman I was coming to see as a canary-eating fairy demon and read the captions over a display of crystals. I could feel her eyes following me, the cat in the shadows, ready to pounce.

About the time I started to scold myself for being a tad bit jealous, the sprite bells signaled another customer.

"Not more questions, I hope," I heard Marci say.

"I need to clear up something with you," said a familiar voice.

Holding a chunk of amethyst in my hand, I turned to see Zeke Owen again, his ID folder open in front of Marci.

"I hear your brother lives with you. Any chance of talking to him?"

"He's gone most of the time. He owns a shrimp boat and lives on it. He's way out in the Gulf right now." She spoke fast, her frail voice no longer under tight control.

"Someone said he was at your trailer night before last."

The coyness returned, full blown. Marci cocked her head and smiled. "Now, Mr. Owen. A lady has her callers."

CHAPTER ELEVEN

I nearly choked on the old-fashioned way of describing a one-night stand. Marci "entertained" gentlemen, I supposed.

"Can you give me the name of your visitor?" Owen asked, but I knew she wouldn't answer.

"Of course not. You're not a policeman, and I don't have to tell you that." She shifted her body away from Owen.

Zeke seemed a bit flustered and glanced toward me. I shrugged. Marci's sleepovers weren't my business. Not yet, anyway.

"We got a missing woman here," he said, the anger control evident in his voice. "She was your former boss and you're not helping a bit."

Marci's eyes got bigger and she stared at him. I could imagine a spell being recited in her head about now.

"You'd best leave," she said.

Owen had nothing to say. His face had turned red. He nodded at me and stomped his big shoes out the door.

"What was that all about?"

"He has this idea that I know what happened to all the Katrina refugees. Silly man. There were hundreds of people who ended up in shelters and other states. The government didn't even bother to track people. How could I possibly know where this woman is?"

"This woman?"

She looked at me suddenly, as though she realized she was actually speaking to me. "I worked at her shop once. That's all. Worked there. I never socialized with her." The anger in her eyes turned to light all of a sudden. "Look! Here's Sheila. She must be feeling better."

I waited for the white haired woman to approach us and figured I'd best get this over with if I wanted to see inside the magic room.

"Oh, hello again. Do you have appointments today or can you squeeze me in for a reading?" I felt like a local at the only beauty parlor in town.

Sheila looked startled for a moment. "Half price for a palm read. I haven't time for the Tarot right now."

"Nor have I," I said and followed her to the little room.

I didn't realize how little. Someone had painted it dark blue and pasted on silver and gold stars and moons. Just behind Sheila's head, a huge white planet Saturn stuck to the wall like a crown. She closed the door, which triggered a tiny pocket light in the ceiling to light up the table area.

She made an "oomph" sound as she sat in her chair. It and the table were draped in dark blue material that matched the walls without the night sky.

"Your palm," she said and took the one I put on the table. She ran her finger around the lines and suddenly let go.

"You see something?" I asked and looked up to see her face sweating profusely within the halo of white hair and blue background.

"Sorry," she said and grabbed a tissue from somewhere below her knee level. "There's something here." She took deep breaths and turned away. Leaning over a trash can, I was sure she'd hurl any minute.

"It can't be that bad," I said.

Sheila took deep breaths and finally sat up straight, dabbing at her sweaty face. "I'm sorry but this presence is saying for you to be careful in the night time. In the dark. There's danger for you there." She broke out in sweat again and stood up. "I'm so sorry, but you must leave now. I need to purify the room."

I wanted to say, "Well, excuse me for living," but I nodded and pulled out some bills from my wallet. She shook her head and continued dabbing at her face.

"No. No charge, just go. Please."

I left and heard her close the door behind me.

"She's got demons today," I said to Marci who seemed surprised at my quick exit.

"She does get them from time to time. That happens when one is a sensitive."

I shrugged and decided to change the subject.

"Do you ever just close up shop and go for a swim or a boat ride?"

"I've been swimming at a beach about three miles from here," she said. "I don't have a boat." She seemed surprised at the question. "Do you?"

"I have a canoe," I said. "And a little camper trailer. I plan to do some exploring on the St. Margaret's. It's not a river I know well." I lied. I may have known the Palmetto better, but I could deal with the boat lanes on the St. Margaret's just as well.

"A canoe! That should be the most fun." It gushed from a woman who sounded like a teenager trying to kiss up to a popular classmate.

"Come by sometime, and I'll give you a ride." I handed her the crystal that was big enough to be a paperweight and pulled out the cash to pay for it. The thought of this ethereal phony in my canoe grated on my nerves.

I left Marci Doucet and her dingling door sprite. Glancing toward Harold's, I saw Pasquin and Harold on their second soda and talking away. Their gravel voices harmonized when they laughed. I headed for the last shop, Mo's Convenience Store.

The in-and-out action picked up here. People from the trailers in Ciel and from the fish camps up and down the river as well as the coast dropped in for supplies. The owner was restocking the beer cooler when I entered. The door had a bell, but this time it was an electric thing rigged to a box.

"Help you?" A short man, thin, with graying temples greeted me. His arms held a crate, and through the tight fit of his tee shirt, I could tell he was mostly muscle. Mo wasn't a big man, but he was no pudgy Zeke Owen.

"Here to pick up some staples," I said. "I'm staying about a week at Ciel. Canoeing." I picked up a plastic basket near the front door.

"You got a canoe?" Mo placed the crate on a stack near the rear door. "I got one you can rent if you don't."

"Yes, I have my own. Do you have many renters?"

He shrugged. "One or two. St. Margaret's ain't too friendly to a canoe. Got to know how to control it on some of the currents."

"Especially when the tide is coming in," I said.

I handed him the basket with peanut butter, crackers, and cans of sardines—fisherman food. It would hold up all day on the water.

Back in front of Mo's, I waved at the two men in front of the junk shop. Pasquin left Harold in his pillowed chair, his chin drooping and his eyes closed.

"You think anyone could go in there and walk off with whatever he wanted. Harold would never know."

"Oh, no." Pasquin shook a finger at me. "Bet nobody puts one over on him. He's like a cat. Wakes at any little disturbance. Knows just what's happening even with his eyes closed."

"And the swamp?"

"Every bit," Pasquin nodded. "Good fellow, really."

"Didn't you say he was in jail at one time?"

"Nam vet. Was all mixed up and got into an armed robbery situation long time ago." He turned toward me. "Done his punishment and had no trouble since."

I nodded and didn't push it anymore. Harold was one of the lost vets from that era, someone who had no focus when he returned to a world that scorned the very idea of that war. Without much help from the government and none from the public, he drifted. Some of the drifting was into crime. It was a story told hundreds of times. I had to trust Pasquin's judgment that Harold was not going to hit him over the head one night for a few dollars. Still, it bothered me that he could become one of the swamp set that got invited to Pasquin's gatherings.

We headed down the familiar road to my house near Fogarty Spring, the Honda protesting with bounces and jerks.

"What's the latest on Jimpson's funeral?"

"We decided not to do anything until they release his body and we get him cremated. No sense in a memorial without the scattering."

That release wouldn't be anytime soon. The case had no suspects and, seemingly, no motive. Forensics would still be running tests.

"Guess you'll have to wait until they let you run the boat procession down the river."

"Too many bones. Too many bodies." Pasquin looked out the window and stayed silent for the ride to Fogarty Spring.

"You plan to stay the night in the trailer?" he asked as I dropped him at his house. "Want me to check your house?"

"Tonight, I'll stay at home," I said. "Vernon may stay at the trailer."

Pasquin saluted and walked through the trees to his porch. I shuddered. Vernon would be close to the shops and in the trailer-park with the fairy vampire. I think I showered the road with dirt spray when I shoved down on the gas pedal.

I worried for naught. Vernon called and said to join him. "I've got some info from the files," he said.

Plato wanted none of leaving him behind at my house. He piled into the car with me and some more supplies. Maybe the trailer-park didn't allow animals, but given the lack of anyone there to oversee the place, how would they know?

Dusk brought some glitter to the camp in the woods. Lights clicked on through the trees where you might not know there was a trailer space. Mo had a small place with a few Christmas lights over the door. It was tucked between tall close pines that swayed in the Gulf breezes enough to play a kind of string music. Where the pines gave way to oaks, several trailers of weekly visitors lined up in rectangular formation, their awnings giving them places to sit and recount fish stories over a shared cooler of beer. They turned on various types of bug lights that probably did no good to keep the mosquitoes from biting. Next to the cooler, you could usually spy a plastic bottle of bug spray for the skin.

Marci Doucet's white trailer was the biggest one there, and the most permanent. Her awning sported hanging chimes and wheels and crosses. They made tinkling sounds with each gust of wind.

She had added another awning at one end to use as a carport. A green minivan sat beneath it, with a dark blue truck behind it.

"A night visitor," I said. Plato looked around at me, then patted his foot on the window.

Vernon hadn't yet arrived. While Plato did his sniffing investigation around the camp, I headed inside the pitiful little camper trailer. The flimsy steps gave me pause, but they held up fine as I opened the door. Looking back, I saw the sensor light pop on and aim at Kayleen's sign. No one would miss that ad.

Inside, I put my bundles on a window seat that doubled as a storage box and living room sofa. To the right was a small built-in formica table with two chairs near a cooking surface and a tiny fridge beneath a row of cabinets. To my left were two narrow beds on either side and a small aisle between that led to the door of the bathroom. From where I stood, it looked about the size of two airplane bathrooms combined.

"And people live long years in places like this," I said and opened the door for a barking Plato. He rushed inside, did some indifferent sniffing and plopped on the sofa. "I'll bet you've been inside this trailer before, right?" He flopped his tail a few times and turned over for a belly scratch.

Plato and I heard the sound at the same time. His ears perked up and most likely mine did, too, at the soft roar of an expensive motor. He rolled over and placed his paws on the window sill. I lifted the curtain. Our trailer was the closest to the old landing on the St. Margaret's. There was no light there. In daylight, a small sign warned against it not being up to code and to use at one's own risk. Someone stood on the boards and waved a flashlight at the approaching boat. It pulled alongside. In faint light, I saw the pilot hold out a hand to someone as he fumbled aboard. As he stood, attempting to balance himself, his face and upper body stood in the beam from the flashlight the pilot now held.

"Zeke Owen," I said under my breath. "Is that who I should beware of in the dark?"

Plato's body became rigid as he gave a soft bark. I placed my hand on his back to keep him from giving us away. It wouldn't take much to shine that flashlight right into the window.

When Zeke had found a seat, the pilot pulled the boat into the open river. Instead of going inland to where the motels were, he turned and headed into the open bay. From there, he could continue into the Gulf—which not many people did in a small boat at night—or turn right to the Palmetto River or left to more camps along the bay.

"Well, what does Sheila and her entity know?" I said and rubbed Plato's sides until he hit the sofa again.

Darkness encased the little trailer camp so that we all looked like fire flies blinking in our spaces. Only the yellow bulbs on high poles and Kayleen's bright light gave the place any kind of guide to approach another trailer. Someone in a distant space sat outside and strummed a guitar. At least he didn't sing. The clearing in the middle was quiet. Gibby was either not at home or had no access to his rum today.

Vernon drove in late. He carried a duffle bag and nothing else.

"I stowed the life jackets inside the canoe," he said. "You're ready for guests."

"No takers," I said and wrapped my arms around him, deputy badge and all. "But the lovely Doucet has expressed an interest."

Vernon hugged me back and chuckled in my ear. "I get the feeling she's not your best friend."

"Don't get me started," I said. "I'm already a bit ticked at my feelings about her."

We ate some tv dinners, warmed in the microwave that took

up most of the counter space. After we took turns in the tiny shower, we lay on the separate narrow beds.

"Isn't this the romantic?" Vernon said. "Wonder if couples really do go on honeymoons in these things."

"Doubt it. They wait until they are older, like the O'Neils. She told me to beware of the dark." I stared at him. "You going to move or shall I?"

Jammed up against the wall didn't cut it. In the end, we both moved to the floor. I don't know if the trailer bounced, but it must not have because Plato slept through it all. I was glad that Pasquin was miles away in his own bed.

With sunlight came Plato's whimpering to go outside. Vernon put cereal together while I dressed and followed Plato. I didn't want him bothering other tenants and calling attention to me. He had scooted somewhere, into the woods probably. I walked the edges of the trees looking for him, a box of treats in my hand. Fishermen had already been up and gone for their daily jaunts on the bay or up the river. Most of their wives would have gone with them. Those that stayed behind drank coffee or something stronger in the early morning humidity. Except for Mo, the shop owners had no need to rise early. The Doucet visitor's truck was still behind her car. Kayleen's sign light had switched off, but inside her trailer, I could see a light where her kitchen window looked over the clearing. The mist in the air was lifting. Plato came running at me from some trees, his tail wagging. He grabbed the treat and headed for the trailer. Vernon came out, dressed, ready to kill in more ways than one. He held the door for Plato, but I nodded that I wanted to stay outside a little longer.

"The place is peaceful this time of morning," he said. "Nice that we don't get the boat traffic here."

I told him about seeing Zeke Owen get on a boat the night

before.

"That reminds me," he said. "I put some printouts on the table for you to read. Just some factual background we found on some of the people here. Tuck them away somewhere when you finish. Maybe your car, away from anyone else who might stay in the trailer."

We didn't kiss like a couple who had spent a warm night together. Public display wasn't good for neighbors or for his fellow deputies to see. They knew about our relationship, but giving them concrete evidence would be like turning on a locker room chatter box.

I wandered a bit after Vernon left. Mr. O'Neil had come out of his travel trailer and sat drinking coffee. The two chairs hadn't moved since I first saw them. Before I could approach him to say good morning, the door slammed open and Sheila stood pale and breathing heavily on the top step. Her wig was missing and bits of wispy gray stood out over her head. Still in a robe, she held out a hand to her husband.

"Need your help," she said and slapped her palm over her mouth.

O'Neil put his cup on the ground near his chair and ran to grab her hand and help her down the steps. He took her behind the trailer, amid thick pines, where she leaned over and vomited. When she stopped, he rushed inside and came out again with a wet towel.

I turned back to feed Plato. Sheila was sick, really sick, not putting on some drama about a presence in the area. Did her reading powers tell her it was coming?

CHAPTER TWELVE

I found that it was easier to walk to the little shops rather than drive along the bumpy road to the front. It took a while, but the path through the pines and oaks finally led to the low coastal scrubs, then to the space between Kayleen's Café and one end of the Talisman. Bub's truck was parked near the café back door and two young boys were unloading boxes.

"Is Kayleen about?" I asked one. He stared at me, said nothing but pointed inside. His dark Indian looks made me think Bub had discovered some day laborers somewhere. I started to ask in Spanish, but decided against it.

I dodged boxes until I found Kayleen bent over one and pulling out dishes.

"These finally arrived," she said. "I was beginning to think we would have to serve on paper plates for the grand opening."

"Aren't you going to hire some help with these?"

"Carol promised to be here, but she got tied up with Gibby again. Lordy, if she does this when she's waitressing, I'll be up a creek." She stood up, rubbed her back, and laughed, "provided I actually have customers." The laugh disappeared. Fear appeared in her face. I suppose it's like this anytime anyone opens a new business. No matter the dream that got you this far, you are asking yourself *what am I doing here?*

"I'm glad to see that Bub is taking an active role," I looked around to watch the two boys carry the breakable goods and sit them gently on the floor. Bub had retreated to his truck to smoke.

"Not so active," said Kayleen. "He was all for this at one time, but the work," she stopped and sighed, "not to mention the opening expense, are getting to him fast."

"He still has his job at the boat yard?"

She nodded. "People aren't renting so many boats anymore, and they aren't getting them repaired much, either. I guess it's the economy." She looked around the kitchen. "I just hope they still like to eat. Even if I get half the crowds Mama gets, I'll break even."

"You're getting seafood off the boats?"

"Yes," this made her smile. "It will be super fresh, and you know how good that tastes. Look," she handed me a menu, "we've got a Cajun section. Not sure how many we'll get here, but we are going to serve their food, too."

I figured she'd get close to none as customers. Maybe some people who liked the Cajun hot food, but she'd end up like Mama, just putting the sauce on the table.

"If you get a lot of the shrimp and oyster crowd, you'll get all kinds. Most will go for the cornmeal fried stuff."

Kayleen nodded. "Long as they pay for it."

"Have any of the shop owners been around to see what you're doing?" I helped her load a stack of dishes into the dishwasher.

"Harold came by a couple of times. He was good to lift a heavy box. Mo is too busy. He never hires any help for that store, and people are always stopping by for something. He promised to hand out flyers for the opening."

"And the two fortune tellers?"

"Sheila's husband dropped by and scanned the main room. He never says much. Strange man, but at least he seems devoted to her. Miss Doucet gushed in here one day. Tried to convince me to buy crystals for each table."

"I don't suppose she gifted you with one?" I figured any spiritual person would bless someone with a good luck charm.

"Not hardly. It's buy or do without where she's concerned. I'd just as soon do without."

The ethereal Miss Doucet hadn't made many friends it seemed. For all their goodness of heart and calling on angels, it was the mercenary side that won.

Bub returned from his smoke break and nodded as he went back to work opening more boxes. The two boys finished their part and sat in the bed of the pickup, swiping at their dripping foreheads. Kayleen noticed and took them sodas.

"Are you excited about the big day?" I asked Bub who wielded the box cutter like he was slicing open a deer carcass.

"Excited? Damn thing is costing me a wad. Everybody wants money up front." He stood up and tossed the cutter onto the next box, slammed his hands on his hips and looked at me. "I hope you know that we're spending all our savings on this place. That's a whole lot of hours being a waiter and fixing boats." He didn't wait for an answer, but grabbed the cutter and sliced away again and again as though he wanted to cut up the merchandise inside the container.

"It will work out," I said, knowing I had no idea what would happen.

"Yeah? You been to that crystal ball lady to find that out? It's like that, you know. Like using a crystal ball and hoping the place will pay."

"Bub, Kayleen is trying so hard. Don't get crazy on her now." I tried to sound casual, but I meant it. A strong negative force in the works was a bad omen, one that had nothing to do with the cards.

"Support?" He nearly shouted. "What does it look like I'm doing?"

"Just do it with somewhat of a smile," I said.

Kayleen returned from the truck and stood over her husband. "I hired those two boys to clean," she said. "We'll need some help, and they're willing to come late, after closing."

Bub didn't look up but grunted and slit one box down the top with one movement.

I said my goodbyes and told them we'd all be there for the opening. "All" would be Pasquin and anyone he brought, Mama, and maybe Vernon with me. Not many if no one else showed.

"Mama is helping with the cooking for that event. She has been so kind to the competition," said Kayleen. She bent to open a box at the same time Bub tossed the cutter on the top. It missed her hand by inches. "That's a dangerous thing to do," she said and glared at her husband.

"Yeah?" Bub turned and grabbed his cigarette pack as he headed out the door.

I moved away and headed through the main room of the new café. It sat peaceful, neat, and nautical. At the moment, it looked comfortable, a place to socialize with fishermen and trailer camp residents and day visitors to the area. This part of the bay was not on the big tourist route that headed for St. George's Island and rented condos. Most of the crowd here would come from the ocean or inland from Tallahassee.

Marci Doucet slipped from the passenger side of the truck that had been parked behind her own car for the night. A man with a deep tanned skin got out of the driver's side.

She unlocked the Talisman door and invited him inside. I let them have about ten minutes, then entered beneath the sprite.

"I want to buy something lucky for the new café owner," I said. "Is it too early to look about the place?"

"Why no," said Marci who was fluffing up her long hair. The man strolled out of Sheila's room.

"Nice," he said and smiled at her. He looked different up close. He wasn't old or worn, just tanned, thin and muscular with a stance of a dancer.

"My brother," she said and smiled at me. "Bernard Doucet. I'm sorry, I never got your name." She smiled at me again.

"Luanne Fogarty." I stuck out my hand and shook Bernard's. Inside all that tan, he had bright blue eyes.

"Bernard has his own boat," she said and straightened some stacks of small books that had Small Spells written on the front. She placed them next to her register. "Shrimp boat," she clarified.

I was surprised. He looked too healthy. Not that shrimpers weren't healthy, but they tended toward too much tobacco and alcohol along with the sun. He had none of the stooped over look from handling nets and equipment.

"Business is good?"

He gave a small laugh and shook his head. He glanced at Marci and made it clear he didn't want to talk. I turned back to some tiny carved statues of gnomes and fairies. I remembered seeing a photo of a boat on one wall and drifted in that direction. There it was. A black and white picture of the ocean and a shrimp boat displaying its rigging. The name on the side read Talisman.

"Just like the shop," I said for them to hear. "I'm assuming this is your boat?"

Bernard stood up straight and frowned at Marci. She placed a hand gently on his arm and smiled.

"Yes, but that photo came from our father who worked the boat before Bernard."

"Is the picture taken on this bay?"

"Not hardly," said Bernard. "It's off Texas, I think. We didn't come this far east until after Katrina."

"You were lucky not to lose it in the hurricane," I said. "So many did."

"Just a stroke of luck being somewhere else when that thing hit."

Bernard picked up a couple of crystal bookends, stared at them as though contemplating buying, then replaced them on the table.

I stared at the blue rock with what looked like barnacles on one side. They gave me an idea.

"If you don't want those," I pointed toward the book ends. "They'd make a perfect gift for Kayleen's counter." I made a scene of leaning close and admiring the deep blue color and the rock and how well it would match both décor and theme of the café.

"Could you wrap them in tissue for me?" I reached for my wallet.

Marci smiled first at Bernard and then at me. She grabbed two sheets of tissue from beneath her counter and draped them over the crystals. With a sweep of both hands she gathered the tissue around them and twisted it beneath the rocks. More tissue and a bag and I had my gift. And not a single fingerprint had been disturbed.

All three of us were smiling as I left. The sprite's bell was really clear today.

The odor of bacon drew me to Harold's Oddities. The big man stood over a hotplate that rested atop a worn table. He cracked an egg and let it sizzle next to the bacon. An automatic coffee pot spurted the last of its brewing exercise.

"Late breakfast?" I asked.

Harold tipped an imaginary hat, and I was reminded of Pasquin's tipping of a real one. "Old man kept me up too late." He laughed and followed it with a cough. "Good company down the Palmetto."

"So you and Pasquin shared the jug last night?" I smiled.

Harold laughed again. "And some other old swamp coots I can't remember. Lots of tales told." He laughed again as though recalling some outlandish feat of man against nature.

"So I've heard," I said.

He lifted the small frying pan in a gesture to ask if I wanted any.

"You go ahead and eat," I said. "I'll wander and ask questions if I see anything interesting."

I heard him chuckle as he turned his back and pulled a dish from somewhere. With bacon and egg in the dish, he picked up a fork and moved to his seat outside. I followed.

"Won't the gnats eat that before you do?" I asked.

"Not if I can help it," he said. He shoveled some egg in his mouth. "What kind of questions you plan on asking? Pasquin told me you're good at that."

I took a seat on something that looked like a stool. "And what else did that old man tell you?"

He gnawed on a piece of thick bacon, his eyes peering at me. "That you dive under the water." He waved the bacon in my direction. "I admire that. Saw men do it in Nam. Only they went under to find bombs—or maybe plant them. I forget. Guess you both ended up doing the same thing."

"Like?"

"Finding dead people." He rested his plate on his knee and stared into the trees. "Always dead people. It just all ends like that, doesn't it?"

A silence came between us. Harold was in a different place, an Asian place where most likely his buddies lay in pieces about the jungle.

"Would you like me to bring you some coffee?"

He jumped and nearly dropped his plate. "That'd be good," he said, "black," and began to nibble on the bacon again.

Inside the shop, I found a huge mug with a handle made in the shape of some kind of flying thing. I poured the coffee and returned it to him.

"Looks like you bought a mug from your neighbor shop."

He laughed then, out of his reverie. "Yes. Figured I could use it even if it did have a flying angel on the handle. It's nice and big."

"Flying angel? I guess I thought it was a fairy or perhaps a good witch."

He took a loud sip of the hot liquid. "It's all what you want it to be. Nothing else. Just what you want it to be."

A group of men entered the shop. I guessed they were from the city since their paleness and big bellies were far removed from the hard working, thin, career boatmen.

"We're looking for crab traps," one said.

Harold shoved the last bit of bacon into his mouth and followed them inside, his flying angel mug in his hand.

I took my bag of book ends and headed in the direction of Mo's convenience store. I had nothing to buy and figured a candy bar would be okay. Before I left Harold's sitting area, I spied Sheila O'Neil getting out of a car and walking toward the Talisman. She had changed herself into the reader again—wig, makeup, folkloric shirt over Capri pants. No one would know she had upchucked her breakfast in the woods behind her trailer.

CHAPTER THIRTEEN

Back in the tiny trailer, I sat at the cold green formica table and sifted through the printouts Vernon had left in a manila folder with no label.

There was Harold with a history of his war years, the robberies and finally a stretch in a Mississippi prison. Released for good behavior, he finally took various jobs in the new casino areas around the coast and finally ended up in one that washed away with the hurricane. He spent weeks in a shelter, helping a church agency with other devastated souls. He opted for a new life here. *And, I guess he got it with his junk shop.* I pushed his sheet back into the file, happy to know he had given Pasquin the truth about his life.

Marci Doucet's life was a bit sketchy. With no prison record, she came across as a Louisiana farm girl who went to public school, did junior college, and worked at various offices until she became a card reader. Her sibling, Bernard Doucet, turned out to be a bit more interesting. He tried amateur bantam weight boxing between hiring out on shrimp boats. His latest endeavor in that area was with a group of boats owned by Tom Kingston. I remembered someone telling me Gibby worked on a Kingston boat and did okay as long as he wasn't rumming it up out there on the high seas. Ben Cardel, the body pulled out of the drink, worked for the same outfit. Not too uncommon since Kingston was a well known boat company that sailed out of this part of the Gulf.

Mo, Morris Miller, of convenience store fame, had done the same thing in several spots along the coast from Louisiana to Alabama. He moved from one store to another as manager. It didn't say if he quit or was fired, just that he took up managing another place. If he had done anything notorious, there was no record of it. Someone had underlined NO CRIMINAL RECORD at the bottom. "Born in Ohio," I said. "He seems to like the Gulf coast better."

I replaced the sheets back into the folder. Staring out the tiny trailer window, I wondered if these three people knew each other, perhaps even working on the same boat. Someone on the park grounds caught my eye. Mr. O'Neil had come from the trees to sit in the beach chair near his trailer. Sheila wasn't with him.

I grabbed two sodas from the half sized fridge and headed outdoors. The mugginess brought out condensation on the bottles, and I had to grip them tightly to prevent dropping them in the sand.

"Hi," I said to the man who had closed his eyes but had his face aimed at the sun. "Would you care for a soda?"

Without moving his head, Mr. O'Neil opened his eyes. For a moment, he froze as though fearing something, but he smiled when he saw me.

"Nice of you." He reached out and took the bottle, motioning for me to take the seat next to him.

"Your wife is reading today?" I sat in Sheila's seat and glanced around me. Tall pines graced the area, and the ocean breezes played through the needles above me. It was a restful spot, possibly good for meditation.

"She is," he said. He smiled after taking a swig and turned to me. "Got a lot of business lately. That man they found dead in the water, he was the husband of one of her clients."

"I heard. Poor Mrs. Cardel."

O'Neil shook his head. "Not so poor. The man was a beast to her, you know."

I sighed. "Yes, I heard that, too. Still, Belinda Cardel seemed a bit out of sorts when the death came."

We sat in silence for a moment. O'Neil gazed through the pine trees as though looking for the sun again. "She'll do better now."

I didn't ask how he knew this. People sometimes have pasts they conjure up when unpleasant situations arise. Maybe the man had an abusive father, or something like that.

"Your wife kept warning her about something to do with water, danger and stuff," I said. "I remember being in the Talisman when Belinda was there. She looked scared to death to me."

O'Neil nodded. "When word got out about Sheila's reading, business picked up." He chuckled almost silently. "Now people want to know about their own lives, even if it's all bad." He turned to me and grinned. "Of course, it isn't all bad for Belinda, is it?"

I had no idea what Belinda's life would be like now that she was free of being socked around when her shrimper came home. Why she stayed around this long would be my question. O'Neil felt that fate had done her a favor, I guessed.

"Does Sheila do this up north, too?"

"Give readings? She played with it for years, mostly at carnivals. When we started roaming the South, she'd find places like fairs to make a few pennies. Sure was happy when the Doucet woman opened her shop. I think we'll be staying here." He paused. "For the duration."

Retirement in a fish camp, living out of a little trailer. It wasn't what I thought would be luxury living, but I lived in a swamp. What did I know?

"Are you ever bothered by Carol Gibson's husband and his demons?" I decided to change the subject.

It worked. O'Neil's face lit up in a big grin. "Never seen a thing like it from a drunk before. He doesn't hit real people, just jabs at the air and yells curses at some imaginary foe. It would be okay, but he tends to make it last the night if somebody doesn't stop him."

"And someone does, I hope?"

O'Neil nodded. "Not sure who it is that calls the sheriff, but somebody does. Mostly for the noise, not so much for his own safety."

"His wife, maybe?"

He chuckled out loud this time. "She finds her own entertainment, and it's not watching her husband fight imaginary devils."

"I guess I'd best not ask anymore about that." I tried to act coy.

"She trots off to help out at the new café." He grinned. "Even before it was a new café."

O'Neil wasn't using names, but I got a nagging hint that really didn't sit right. Was Carol Gibson getting it on with Kayleen's husband? In the recesses of my mind, I saw the demise of Kayleen's Café if such a discovery popped up one day.

"Has Sheila ever done a reading for Kayleen?"

O'Neil jerked his head toward me and frowned. He slowly shook his head. "She never asked for one."

I stood up and took the two empty soda bottles. "Well then, let's hope the fates have good things in store for the place. Sheila warned me against being in the dark. I guess I'd best tend to things in the daylight."

O'Neil nodded and gave a half wave as I strolled back to my trailer. As I opened the door and glanced back, I saw he had his face in both hands as though praying or meditating, maybe crying?

Like some swamp phantom, Plato appeared at my heels as I opened the door. "How do you do that, old dog?" He headed for his water dish and splattered the linoleum floor. I handed him a treat and sat in the same chair by the window.

I was restless. Clouds accumulated and darkened the little sunlight that came through the heavy tree growth. I took a chance and called Marshall Long's office. Someone picked up the receiver, and I heard a loud sip. He was taking a soda break, one of many during his day with body parts.

"Do you have anything on the bones we found?" I asked, knowing I had no official role in this end of the investigation.

"Just that the skull probably belongs to the arm bones from the coat." His sip had hit bottom.

"I thought there was speculation that the skull was male and the arms might be female."

"Skull is male. So are the arms. It's a small male, not a midget, just a short, small boned fellow. Got some DNA but we don't have it all back yet."

"How do you know the skull and arms belong to each other?"

"Don't. I said probably. Bone quality, color, stuff like that—not to mention they were both found in the same body of water." He took one last labored sip of the cola, sounding as though he'd bring up the paper cup bottom. "Look, Luanne, this is educated guessing. Don't quote me."

"You wouldn't know any more on Jimpson, would you?"

"What's the matter? Things slow at the fish camp? How about finding a rod and reel, dig some worms, and catch a few."

"For a flash moment, I thought a pile of student essays might help pass the time."

"Ha! Go paddle a canoe, Luanne."

"Look, Marshall, can you do a fingerprint search for me? It's sort of related to this case, and Tony did say to keep an eye on people here."

"What have you got?" Marshall's voice became cautionary like it always did when he was about to say no.

"Some bookends handled by someone who seems like he could be someone else."

"Not sure about that. Does Tony know?"

"Okay. Let's forget it for now. Vernon is looking into the backgrounds of people here. Maybe he can convince Tony."

Things were slow at the fish camp. I looked at Plato who sensed the observation and looked back at me. He began to slap his tail on the floor as though working up a rhythm toward action.

"Want to take a walk, old dog?" I looked back at the phone. "Not you, Marshall."

In spite of the threat of rain, I wandered down the path from the fish camp and onto the small road toward the shops. Plato trotted along, with detours into the trees to smell something of interest.

There was no traffic going in and out of the camp on this road. I walked in silence except for the occasional breeze through the pines or crack on the ground twigs beyond the road. Plato stopped once and stared into a thick growth of palmettos and barked. He lost interest and ran on ahead of me. I caught up with him at the rear of the junk shop.

"Your old dog done found him a comfortable seat," said Harold.

"He'll find a nice meal if you let him," I said and took a seat without an invitation. "Does this life suit you?"

Harold turned his head toward me. "Do I look unsuited?" He didn't wait for an answer, but raised his eyes to the sky. "I'm a worn out veteran. Been worn out since I left Nam, maybe even before I left. That place tore holes out of a fella's soul, and I don't mean gun holes." He stared at the sky a while longer then looked at me. "Yes. This life suits me. Nobody shoots me here. And I don't have to shoot anybody else. See all this?" He waved toward the shop. "It's junk. I make a bit of living to add to my pension, but if some nutcase with a pistol wanted to steal it, what would I care? It's not worth defending. And, you know what? That's what suits me. Things that aren't worth defending. Don't give me some jewelry or new clothing, stuff that would cost me dearly if I lost it. I know about loss, and I don't like it." He sighed. "And don't give me another country to defend, either."

We sat in silence. I had heard stories both about and from Vietnam vets and they all seemed bizarre in their way. This one, I hadn't heard.

"You would defend your life, wouldn't you?"

"Maybe."

I bid Harold goodbye and let him know that Plato would leave when he felt like it. Harold stared at the dog for a moment and smiled. They both closed their eyes.

Mo's store had three customers: two young boys buying fish hooks and Zeke Owen.

I wanted to hear Owen. Making my way near the two boys, I took an interest in their selections.

"Where are you two planning to fish?" I picked up some lures, pretending to admire their designs.

"In the river," one said in an excited preteen voice. The other nodded and gave me a quick glance.

"What kind of poles are you using?" I never took up fishing as a hobby the entire time I'd lived on the Palmetto River, but they didn't know that.

"Our grandpa is going to show us how they used homemade poles when he was a kid," the other, slighter and perhaps younger one, said. "We'll have more fun than on the boat out in the ocean."

"Yeah, that got boring, and we got too sunburned." The first boy lifted his tee shirt sleeve to show the difference between his red and white skin.

"You've got a boat, then?"

"My dad does. He keeps it at the Crusty Dock down that way." He pointed somewhere in the direction of Kayleen's Café.

"Do you know why they named it Crusty?" The first boy had my attention and he wasn't going to let go. "It's because they have lots of crabs and shrimps around there, and they're called crusta-ceans. That's where they get Crusty from, but they have mollusks, too. If you go to the shore and wait for a wave, then let the wave go back, you see lots of little clams going into the sand. You can take both hands and dig down and get them out." I felt his ex-citement. It was something I did a million times as a child, like finding live treasure.

"Yeah," said the other boy, "and the clams are all different colors. We collect them." He grinned at me and turned to his companion. "Only you have to be careful not to put them in your room when you first catch them. They'll stink after a while."

I joined their laughter. "Sounds like you fellows know your seafood."

I took the opportunity to move away, closer to Owen who was stuffing a canvas bag with canned goods. He looked up briefly at me and nodded.

"Looks like you're going fishing, too," I said, and stared at his bag.

"Something like that," he said and scurried off to the register where he unloaded everything for Mo.

The boys ran to the register with a packet of hooks and fidgeted while Owen paid his bill. While they were paying, I drifted toward the door and watched Owen get into a Jeep. The driver wasn't someone I had ever seen.

"Grandpa is waiting," said one boy as they ran out the door. They piled into an old pickup and the driver who, I suppose, was Grandpa, drove them back toward the river.

I paid for a six pack of cola and bought a tin of sardines and some crackers.

"You must be fishing, too," Mo chuckled. "Got the standard sea faring supplies."

"Not quite. No beer." I smiled back at him.

"Good for that. I've seen too many people swig it down, then fall to the depths. Not a pretty sight." He passed the bag over to me.

"You've been around fishermen a while, then?" No one else was in the store. I figured I could do some small talk.

"Oh, yeah. Plenty of family went in for the day on the river or the ocean, soaking up alcohol and sun, catching just about nothing. Never cared much for it myself, not after a cousin fell into the ocean and was washed up to shore the same afternoon. Skunk drunk. His friends weren't much better off, had no idea how to rescue him. They just tossed him a life ring. It washed on shore about a mile away about the same time."

"Then why did you choose to stay around water?"

"Money maker. These kinds of stores do well most any place, but near fishermen's camps, work is steady. Especially in places where the weather is good all year." He saluted me and turned to opening some supplies, his cue that he'd revealed enough about his life. It surprised me that he praised the steady work and not the steady sales, like keeping busy was the goal.

I took my drinks and bag and headed toward Kayleen's. Two ladies in Bermuda shorts sat in folding beach chairs outside The Talisman. Through the window, I saw others standing around collections of scented candles and amulets.

"Busy today," I said to the women. One was fanning herself with a Kayleen's Café flyer.

"It's the reader who's busy," she said. "We've got appointments, but I'm burning up in this heat."

"Worth waiting for," said the other who refused to make eye contact with me.

I moved on, not wishing to see the silly women—and they all seemed to be women—pay out money to have their fortunes read based on the prediction Sheila had given the Cardel woman.

Kayleen was taking a rest between food deliveries.

"I have to take the goods when the boats get them into dock," she said. "So far, I've got mullet and grouper, but the fresh oysters and scallops are still to come."

"Fresh? Already shucked?"

"No, I've hired two teenagers to shuck as needed. They came recommended by some shrimpers."

"I hope they work out," I said, not asking what she planned to do when school started in the fall. "In fact, I really hope this place does a booming business. You and Bub have worked too hard to have it fail."

She glanced at me. "Well, I have." She sat in silence. I didn't know what to say. It wasn't exactly praise for her husband. She smiled then and looked at me. "He has, in his way. Works really hard down at the boat repair dock to bring in enough money for this to work."

"You're all set with kitchen help, cleaners, waiters and such?"

She laughed. "Why? Are you applying for a job?"

CHAPTER FOURTEEN

Applying for a job? I laughed as I drove toward Crusty Dock. Kayleen's question gave me the cue to walk back to the trailer with my purchases. Once there, I couldn't stand the quiet. O'Neil wasn't in his chair. Nothing stirred, and Kayleen's big sign just emphasized her words. They hadn't been kind, I didn't think. Not even joking. Facetious, maybe? Something bothered me. That's when I piled into the Honda and headed down the two-lane highway to see dead fish arrive.

This was where locals and others with sea-going private boats docked after a long day on the bay. Further down the coast, bigger shrimp boats docked with their catch and unloaded it into refrigerated houses and trucks. The entire area was strung with lights that lit up like a Christmas tree at night since many of the boats waited until after dark to come ashore.

I parked on the oyster shell covered area beside trucks that I knew belonged to those out on the water. A few boats were tied up, belonging to fishermen who couldn't get the day off from their city jobs. A water lane ran from the dock area inland to another dock and boat ramp. A worn wood building with a tin roof sat at the end. Over a wide door, wide enough to haul in a fishing boat, a sign read CRUSTY DOCK BOAT REPAIR. Even from where I stood in the parking lot, I could hear men's voices coming from the massive interior.

A man in what looked like expensive boating pants and shirt came through the door space. He carried something in his hand, possibly a part he either had repaired or replaced by the mechanics. He headed for the pier where a man sitting next to a wood post sipped a beer. It was Zeke Owen. He wore a baseball cap, but his skin still appeared sunburned. He said something to the other man and joined him. They headed to the end of the pier and boarded a large fishing boat. Whoever piloted it, took it into the bay and headed for open ocean.

There wasn't much room to stroll on this part of the coast. It was meant for industry, not tourism—except for those who owned boats. I strolled down one of the wooden piers. Most of the slips were empty this time of day, but a few tied up fishing boats of all sizes. One of the bigger ones had a party happening on deck, complete with a circle of chairs, a cooler, and a television set. Four men drank beer and watched a golf tournament, making me wonder if they wanted to fish or golf. I decided what they really wanted to do was drink and left them to it.

There was nothing to see on the water, and I turned back to look at the buildings on shore. From where I stood, I could see one side of the boat repair shop where the employees had parked their cars. Bub's truck was there, recognizable from its slightly beat up appearance. *At least he's not with Carol Gibson or Miss Doucet today,* I thought. The second image played in my head and made no sense. The ethereal spirit of Marci Doucet coupling with the heavy smoking and rough edged Bub Romaine made no sense. Maybe I was wrong.

I spied a door on the side of one of the buildings that received seafood from the big boats. A sign read SEAFOOD WHOLESALE TO THE PUBLIC. A tiny woman with a headscarf sold me some lovely bay scallops. "Sweeter than deep ocean ones," she promised.

As I drove back to the trailer camp, I could see heavy clouds far out over the bay. It would be stormy out there and maybe reach shore soon, an ominous warning that not even here were these washed out refugees safe from the elements.

Back in the little trailer, I rediscovered just what an all-thumbs cook I was. I found a tiny skillet, some garlic salt, cooking oil and a package of rice. My plan was to saute the scallops and serve them over rice. The salad would have to be tomatoes. I hadn't remembered lettuce.

At six, Vernon phoned to say he was on his way. By the time I had the rice done and the scallops sizzling in the pan, he called again to say he'd be delayed.

"Something came up," he said. "I'm to meet Tony at Mama's Table."

He would eat great Southern food at Mama's Table and I was stuck with my own concoction—even if it was a fresh one. I looked outside and saw Mr. O'Neil in his chair again. Sheila wasn't there.

I covered the scallops and drifted outdoors. It was still light and none of the storm clouds had come this way. The fishermen weren't in yet.

"Is Sheila still busy?" I asked.

O'Neil looked up and didn't seem to recognize me at first. "Oh, yes. She's got some private readings tonight. Miss Doucet gave her a key to the back door."

"Well, it seems work has put us both in a lonely position," I said. "And I just made some lovely scallops. Would you care to join me?"

He looked surprised and frowned. I thought he was going to say no, but he stood up and nodded. On the way to my trailer, he said, "I don't often get an offer like this."

"I don't often cook, either," I said. "This is kind of an old stand-by. Hope you don't expect much."

He piled butter onto the rice and topped it with scallops. Lining up his tomatoes, he sprinkled them with pepper. "Great stuff," he said and ate steadily.

"Do you and Sheila ever buy local fresh seafood?"

He shook his head. "She wouldn't know what to do with it. And I surely wouldn't. We just buy stuff for the microwave or go out. That place up the Palmetto River is nice."

He meant Mama's Table, and nice wasn't what Mama would call a compliment. "Let's hope Kayleen's will be as nice," I said.

"Opening can't be too soon," he said. "We'll be going often." He took a sip of the iced tea I had made and frowned. "Any sugar?"

I handed him some packets out of a box. "You like sweet tea, then?"

"It's funny down here," he said as he stirred three packets of sugar into his glass. "You go to a restaurant and ask for iced tea, and they ask if you want sweet or unsweet."

"I guess up north you get it sweet?"

"No, unsweet, always. Or not at all. You ask for tea, it might be brought in a cup, steaming hot."

"I guess you and Sheila really prefer it hot."

He stopped for a moment and stared into his plate. "She doesn't like cold drinks much at all anymore. And her tea and coffee have to have gallons of sugar in it. Used to be, she'd drink both black." He shrugged and shoveled in another spoon of rice.

"Can her stars explain her change of taste," I tried to be humorous.

"No. The stars haven't predicted much for her." He went quiet, not even smiling at my attempt to keep things light.

After O'Neil ate a bowl of melon and bananas, he sat back and nodded at me. "That was great. Freshest food I've had in a few days."

"I'm sorry there isn't any left to send to Sheila." I was also sorry there wasn't any left for Vernon until I remembered he'd be full of all kinds of seafood from Mama's Table.

"No, no. Sheila only eats big on some occasions. Mostly, she goes to bed after a bowl of cereal. I try to get her to eat better, but she says she's just not hungry."

I bid him goodbye, and he strolled across the open space to his trailer. He didn't go inside, but sat in his chair and stared into the twilight. When the camp security lights came on, he was still there. I supposed he was there to wait for Sheila to return.

I heard a splash in the river behind the little trailer and ventured around the end. Mullet often jumped high in the air, giving humans a thrill of seeing acrobatic fish. The security lights barely lit up the shore, but I knew the slow slide of a gator into water when I heard it. I shuddered. Was this part of Sheila's warning about darkness? Stepping on a gator wasn't likely to happen, but a gator grabbing a dog for supper wasn't uncommon. I moved a bit closer to the water and saw the nose and eyes of the reptile moving through the water, the security lights flashing against them for a few seconds.

To my relief, Plato had drifted back by the time Vernon opened the door. They greeted each other and sat down heavily, both weary from the day's work.

"Tony says just about the entire department is coming to this grand opening," Vernon said. He laid his gun belt on the floor at one end of the couch. "He's got a hunch that Jimpson's killer came from down here. Seems they found a few oyster shell remnants where footprints should be inside the bait shop."

"Oyster shells are used all over the area in lots and gardens. Why are they from here?"

"Seems they've got some scallop and clam shells mixed in with them. We tried to come up with places that toss all kinds into the lots, and mostly they are places near the unloading centers."

I grabbed my sandals from the tiny closet near the beds and turned them upside down. "There are shells stuck in these rubber soles, but I see only oysters."

"It's Marshall Long and his lab work. He did scrapings from the floor and found the shell mix." Vernon sighed. "Anyway, Tony says it's a place to start. Look at the people close to the bay and Crusty Dock. Of course, some jerk could have come in all the way from Apalachicola and left the evidence."

"Or Carabelle."

He shrugged again. "Humor us, Luanne."

I tossed my shoes back into the closet and snuggled next to him. "I'll humor you, only you." I hesitated, then asked, "Can you get some fingerprints lifted off some bookends? It's just another hunch that needs humoring." I grabbed the bag of bookends and placed it in his lap.

"I'll see what I can do," he smiled. "Leave them where I won't forget them in the morning."

"Okay. Now I'll really humor you."

"With or without burrs," he said and pulled one of the sticky things from his pants legs. "I've been through the woods today, the ones around Jimpson's store. K-nines picked up a scent that led all through the trees and bushes and back out to another part of the river." He leaned over and rubbed Plato's head. "Damned dogs."

"The shower is all yours," I said, and helped him unbutton his shirt.

Late into the night, I lay awake and stared at the shadows the trees made in the moonlight against the trailer walls. Vernon snored lightly, and Plato whimpered a few times. Not far away, I heard a truck pull in and stop. Plato jumped when I got up to look out the window. The big security light still lighted up the sign and the truck that had parked in front of Kayleen's trailer. Bub was leaning against the driver's door, smoking. He nodded toward a man who came from the other side of the truck and passed him on the way to Marci's trailer. There was no vehicle near. I figured he'd either walked or came with Bub. His tall stance gave him away as Bernard Doucet, the handsome brother of the lovely Marci. I had visions of the Doucet family. Two handsome parents producing handsome children. "A pretty witch and a shrimper," I whispered in the dark. Plato answered with a couple of slaps of tail. "A bantam weight boxer?" I remembered the papers that described one of Bernard's early adventures. "Can you be tall for that?"

I heard a car door slam and someone yell "take it easy." Someone came running from the road that led to the shops and stood in the middle of the clearing.

"Damn you, Gibby," said Bub who stamped out his cigarette butt. "You're not going to pull one of your loud nights."

Gibby lifted a bottle of liquor and took a long swig, bending his back as far as he could go without falling. He came up coughing and laughing. Without taking a step, he let out an Indian war whoop that must have been heard two miles up the river. He began to dance, singing nonsense syllables over and over. Plato was on his feet now and threatening to bark. He made urgent little woofs and paced at the door.

I lifted the scruffy animal to the window and allowed him to watch with me. His front paws rested on the narrow sill, and his ears stood at attention. The tiny woofs continued.

"Crazy man about to become crazier," I said.

Gibby had short, stubby arms and legs, but they were powerful enough to fling through the air and keep his balance. He swigged again and sang louder, but with the gusto of a man who had seen dancing fairies, not demons. It didn't last long. Bub turned to go inside his trailer when Gibby let out a long trill of screech owl sounds.

"Damn bastard! Go to bed!" Bub stared at the man.

Gibby stared back for a moment and started a sing-song of "Noooooo, nooooooooo!" He took the last of the rum from the bottle and flung it hard against Bub's truck. A piece of paint flew into the light.

"You…" Bub ran to the side and looked at the dent. He turned and began his own slur of curses at the drunk man.

Gibby had found his demon in this bottle of rum and began flailing about with his short arms, boxing at visions coming from the direction of Bub's voice. He staggered but never fell, only turned in circles, poking hard at the space above and in front of him. When Bub ran out of words, Gibby took up the shouting with curses even worse than Bub's. He dared Chinamen to fly down and toss fire at him, to turn him into a chicken who couldn't run. He made Indian sounds and danced around an imaginary fire.

All the while, Bub was touching the dent in his truck. His anger thoroughly saturated, he turned and yelled at Gibby. "Just get close to me you stupid sothead. I'll give you a demon to fight. You'll feel him this time." He held up a fist.

Gibby didn't need a second invitation. He stuck out both arms. With fists balled he ran straight to Bub and belted him time after time in the gut. Bub folded. For all his anger, he hadn't really expected the drunk to be so strong and accurate. He made one attempt to put one arm up against his foe. Gibby gave it a strong whack and a bone cracked. The cries came up even louder then, Bub in pain, Gibby in triumph over the devil.

"I need to call someone," I said to Plato. I turned to see Vernon rising off the bed and reaching for his gun.

"What the hell...?"

"No guns," I said and placed the call. "It's the local drunk and I think he's broken someone's arm this time."

Lights flickered on in trailers and people stood at windows and doors. Carol Gibson made an appearance and yelled at her husband. "The law is going to come again and this time, I'll let them take you!"

She looked backwards into her trailer for a moment and ran into the clearing. Vernon had pulled on pants and a shirt and met her there. The two of them held the man down by his shoulders while his feet and legs thrashed about and kicked up dirt. I had dressed and rushed out to see about Bub. Plato followed and took up a frantic barking and running back and forth at Gibby. The drunk really did think a demon beast was after him now and began screaming in terror. I comforted Bub as best I could, telling him not to move the arm. Gibby had slugged his forearm. The break was bad enough to distort the shape. His face grew pale and he breathed in short gulps.

"Man, it hurts," he said.

I held onto his other side and kept reassuring him an ambulance would come soon. I was close enough to smell the cigarette remnants and his own supply of demon rum.

"Tell Kayleen to get out here," he gasped.

I looked at the dark trailer. Patting Bub on his good side, I went to the door and knocked. No answer.

"Is there a key?"

He made a gesture to his shirt pocket. I retrieved the keyring and opened the door. Inside, nothing moved when I turned on the light. Things looked clean, in place, except some recent small boxes with deliveries of spices. In the bedroom area, the beds were still made.

No one was home.

CHAPTER FIFTEEN

The little fish camp in the woods lit up worse than Christmas with sheriff cars flashing blue lights, flood lights turned onto the clearing, and every trailer in the place with their inside lights—except Bub's. I turned those off when I couldn't find Kayleen.

Bub just gave a bewildered look when I said she wasn't there. His focus was on his pain. "A compound fracture," said the EMT who packed him off to the emergency clinic in Palmetto Springs.

Gibby never stopped lashing out, even when the deputies cuffed him and tucked him in the back seat of a patrol car. He even used his head to bat against the seats. Carol Gibson stood with her arms folded, many feet from her husband, her face frowning with anger.

"I'm not bailing him out," she told the arresting officer. "You keep him until he's sober. Then I'll decide if he can come back here." When they drove off with the screaming man, she tossed up her hands and sat on her trailer steps.

"Sometimes, I wish that hurricane had just taken him into the water and pushed him to the depths." She put her hands over her face. "I cannot stand it another minute."

Sheila had joined the melee, her terry cloth robe looking several sizes too large. She moved toward Carol and placed an arm around her.

"Now, now. Remember what I told you. Your troubles will

be over. Bear with them for now. You'll not be defeated by them."
She stroked the woman's hair.

"So Carol Gibson was one of Sheila's customers," I said to
Plato. I held him back or he would have insisted on exploring all
the feet that trampled the clearing. He looked up at me for interpretation. "She's going to have to get it together soon if she plans
to be a good waitress."

Vernon came toward me. "We tried Kayleen's cell phone. It's
turned off, it seems. No answer there or on the café phone. You
want to take a ride over there?"

Plato piled into the patrol car with me, Vernon, and the deputy
who drove. That's when I felt the tension. They had asked around
the trailers. Kayleen was always at home this time of night. Everyone had hoped she was working late on the opening and ended
their thoughts with *yes, that had to be it.*

The café was dark except for security lights at the corners. I
held Plato back while the two deputies walked around the building.

"No sign of a break-in," said Vernon. "I got the key from
Bub. Let's see what's inside. He ordered Plato to stay in the car.
The dog obeyed, but his legs would fly the minute the door opened.

"The alarm may go off," said Vernon as he stuck the key in
the lock.

He was right, something like an up-close fog horn began blasting
into the quiet coastal night. Plato began barking and jumping about
the patrol car.

A light came on from one corner of the dining area. The three
of us stood inside the door, next to the new counter where people
would pay for take-out, when we heard shouts—male and female—come from a storage room. A naked woman with a pillow ran to a panel and punched a code.

Kayleen stood before us inside her new café. She was pale from the shock. Realizing her state, she gripped her arms around the pillow to hide her front and jumped behind the counter.

"What is going on?" She glanced down at herself to make sure she had covered her chest.

"You tell us," said the deputy who suppressed a grin.

Vernon shot him a warning and said, "Bub's got his arm broke in a fight with Gibby. We couldn't find you. He's on his way to the clinic in Palmetto Springs."

Kayleen stared in horror that turned to anger. She lifted one hand, exposing a breast, and pounded the counter. "Damn that man! I knew he'd screw this up. I just knew it."

Everyone's eyes turned away from Kayleen's attempt to cover the exposed breast and toward the storage room again. A man stood there. He would have been nude, too, but had taken a moment to tie a shirt about his waist.

"Hello Bernard Doucet," I said. "Does your sister know you're out?"

When it was all over, Vernon said no crime was committed unless you considered the religious one of adultery, which the local sheriff's office didn't, and Kayleen needed to get dressed and get to the clinic. He didn't say anything to Bernard, just nodded as the now dressed man walked out the door and headed for the camp. The deputies didn't offer him a ride.

Kayleen stood her ground. Once dressed, she stuck out a finger and said, "I was working late on the opening. I really was. Bernard was helping and things just got out of hand. But I WAS working late. Is that clear?"

"What you do in your working late time," said Vernon, "is between you and Bub. I won't tell him." He looked at us and we nodded. I knew what would happen at the sheriff's office. Every inch of Kayleen's rather well put together body would be discussed in all its glory. Bub may not hear it, but the rest of the world would know how Kayleen inaugurated her new café.

Carol Gibson filed papers the next day. She had a job now and figured she could do without Gibby stirring up the park every time he came home from a shrimping job. "Even county welfare would give me food and shelter. What do I need that aggravation for?" She screamed at the elements as she packed up his clothes and sat the boxes outside the trailer. Their pitiful awning would protect them from a drizzle but not a downpour, not even from the incessant humidity. If Gibby didn't get out soon, he'd have mildew for wear.

Bub came home later in the day with a heavy cast on his arm and pain killers in his system. He couldn't lie down. He rested in a chair and smoked until he started to hurt again. He popped another pill and slept, then woke up and smoked some more. When Kayleen came home, she led him outside to a chair next to his dented truck, where he smoked and popped more pills. No one saw him eat, but we assumed Kayleen had given him something.

Marci Doucet left early for her shop. I was sipping strong coffee after the fitful night when I saw her leave. She wore her streaming scarf top, a violet one this time, over Capri jeans. There was no sign of her brother. "Maybe she doesn't care what he does," I said to myself. Half expecting to hear Plato's tail slap the floor, I realized he hadn't returned from his morning outing.

I opened the door to the trailer and gazed into the clearing. Had he been around the area, he would have come running. I returned to the tiny formica table and finished off the pot of coffee. My tiny abode was beginning to close in on me. "How do these people live like this?" I didn't make a guess, but got up and strolled outside. Wind blew through the pine tops, the kind of wind that signaled a rainstorm in the summer. I looked at the trailers, mostly minuscule things that had seen better days. The vacationers parked theirs, but the long timers used concrete blocks to prop them higher than the tires. Each one had a vehicle parked somewhere nearby, giving the whole place a feeling of haphazard about to turn to junk. "I need to go home," I said under my breath.

Instead of jumping into the car and aiming it toward Fogarty Spring, I headed for my canoe. It hadn't been used yet, and since I'd given that as an excuse to be in the park, I decided it was time.

The currents were running strong. I slipped on a life jacket and tossed the other one to the back. I rowed up river until I reached a lane that would take me to the bayou where they found Cardel's body. The tide was coming in here, too, and I could almost feel the canoe rise with the water. The lane was lined heavily with ancient oaks whose limbs draped over the water. I had to dodge them in a zig-zag pattern until I came to the bayou. It circled a tiny island, just a patch of land sticking above the water, really. Maybe someone who was stranded would go on it, but it had no use otherwise. "What was Cardel doing there?" Oaks packed the river banks, their roots exposed in some spots on the high muddy walls. There were no trees on the little island, just high grass and mud. I moved the canoe closer, disturbing an egret that flew upward from the grass and placed itself on the river bank. "I'll bet there are nests all over this area."

Turning back, I pushed through the lane again. This time, I met some kayakers. They rode in boats that were exactly alike with a company logo on the side.

"Are those rentals?" I asked as I waited near overhanging branches for them to pass.

"Yeah. Place up the St. Margaret rents them out," yelled one man with huge arms. "They got canoes like yours, too, and motor boats."

I nodded. I knew the place. When you rented a space in the fish camp, the clerk gave you some flyers that advertised places like boat rentals.

Back at the camp, I pulled the canoe next to the trailer and secured the oars and life jacket. The winds had brought the clouds. Lightning flashed in the distance. It would be seconds before it was right on us, flooding the clearing and washing away all signs of last night's fiasco.

Plato came running down the road that led from the shops. He darted into the trailer just as a loud clap of thunder rattled the entire camp.

I watched from the little window as O'Neil ran from his trailer and folded the two chairs, dragging both inside. He had left the door ajar. Sheila stood there watching him, her wig missing and revealing the scanty hair. She wore what looked like a white night gown. The only color about her was the darkness around her from the interior and the gray shadows around her eyes. I was reminded of a famous painting I once saw of a woman in a nightmare.

Lightning flashed with a fury. Plato pushed himself as far beneath the formica table as he could get. I crossed my fingers that the trailer was grounded. The rain came down in a fury, driving spikes of water into the clearing and turning it all to mud. It was a familiar sight, not unusual in this state, at least not until I saw Sheila emerge from her door.

She was still in the white gown. Her feet were bare. She walked into the clearing and turned circles, shouting something that couldn't be heard over the pounding rain. Lightning flashed, but she didn't run from it. She stopped and turned her face upward, her arms out in an almost religious stance of accepting the Holy Ghost. The flimsy hair strands were nothing but streaks now, and her gown clung to her aging body.

"She could be struck," I said. I guess the urgency was in my voice, because Plato jumped from his hiding place and began to bark. It was a futile bark. Nothing like it could be heard over the noise of the rainstorm.

Even with the danger of lightning, I figured I'd better do something. An umbrella would be useless in this storm, and I had no raincoat here. I decided I'd best just go out and escort her back inside her place. Before I could get the door open, O'Neil rushed into the storm and pulled on his wife's arm. She tried to resist but soon gave up and returned with him.

Plato stopped barking and sat at my feet. "What was she doing, old dog? Getting some kind of divine inspiration from the elements?" It didn't look like that. It was more like a crazy woman. "Maybe readers, or seers, are kind of crazy." I scratched Plato's ears. "What do you think, old boy?"

In less than an hour, the rain with all its drama moved on toward Tallahassee where it would storm on the nice homes and government buildings then, like a wandering lover, visit southeast Georgia until it hit the Atlantic. Behind, it left a mud field in the clearing. Until the hot sun dried the space between the blades of grass, it would be like walking through soup. Thinking of Gibby stomping his demons in this mud, I glanced toward Carol's trailer. The boxes of clothes were soaked, dark mud surrounded their bottoms. One had broken loose and sat in a mud puddle a few feet from the protection of the awning. It would not be a pretty homecoming for the man. It got even uglier when I saw a locksmith truck pull up near the clearing. He headed for the Gibson trailer.

Vernon showed up finally. My cabin fever dissipated some-what when he smiled at me and handed over two bags of take-out from Mama's Table.

"She sent grouper fingers and all the extras," he said. "She'll be around tomorrow for the opening."

I'd almost forgotten it was time for the big event at Kayleen's Café.

"Bub won't make it, I guess," I said and glanced outside. "He smoked in a chair out there until the storm came." I told Vernon about Sheila's rain communion and the lock changes on the Gibson trailer.

"This place is like a soap opera," he said. "Any sign of the Doucet brother?"

I shrugged. "Didn't see him, but the storm was heavy and he could have been inside. His truck is still there."

Vernon smiled at me. "You're really getting to be the snoopy old lady, aren't you?"

I glared at him. "Open the food and let's eat."

During the welcome repast of fried fish, grits, hushpuppies, slaw, and iced tea, we talked about what was happening with Jimpson's body.

"No funeral until Long is finished and the sheriff says to let it go," said Vernon. "The knock on the head looks a lot like the one on Cardel's head. Tony is operating on the idea that there is one killer."

"Motive?"

"Can't figure that one out," he said.

"Suppose Cardel was killed and somehow Jimpson witnessed it," I took a bite of a hushpuppy.

"Could be, but the bodies weren't near each other at discov-ery. And, they don't seem to have been moved. Cardel is harder to tell."

"He could have been dumped."

"Yes, but somebody would have had to get him to the bayou, or Jimpson would have had to be in that area to have seen it."

"Would Jimpson have a reason to be there?" The old man was like Pasquin. He could have been anywhere on the river. It was what they did.

"He sells bait. Might be some small fish he nets around there to use." Vernon picked up a grouper finger and leaned back, nibbling on it and dropping corn meal particles on his chest. "Lots of bird nests on that little land area. Maybe he was checking on them."

It wouldn't have been too farfetched for one of the swamp denizens to make sure the birds weren't being disturbed. But it would have been a simple row-by and look, not a venture onto the land like a wildlife agent would do.

"Anymore news on the bones?"

"Marshall Long says the DNA is still at the lab, but he's thinking the head and arms belong to each other. The question on that one is were the bones dumped at sea and washed in or were they dumped closer to the site of discovery."

CHAPTER SIXTEEN

The big day arrived with the clearing still muddy from the storm. All the shop owners and Kayleen were out early. The local papers had run small articles about the opening of a new coastal restaurant where you could eat hot Cajun or cornmeal-dipped catfish. After filling your belly, you could walk down the way and have your fortune read, buy some organic soap, shop for iron antiques, or just pick up a six pack and drink in the shade. Not bad for a short outing to the bay.

Bub sat outside, one arm still in its cast, the other supporting his cigarette. Beside his chair, Kayleen had placed a cooler and filled it with beer. His bottle of pain killers rested on top of the cooler. She wasn't going to take any chances of having him around for her party. He'd be on substances for most of the day.

"Do you think she'll send over some lunch?" asked Vernon, looking at the poor man whose unshaven face showed terrific pain.

"I'll be sure to ask," I said. I opened the door for Plato who shot outside and disappeared into the trees. "I think he visits Harold's when he's not here."

"If that dog could only talk." Vernon ran a hand over his bald head, perhaps a habit from days when he had some hair. He placed the deputy sheriff hat on his head and strapped on his gun.

"Did you find anymore about the Doucet family?"

"Nothing. Why?"

"It's just that Bernard Doucet is not what I'd call bantam weight. Not that I know anything about boxing. He's supposed to own a boat called The Talisman, like his sister's shop. Can it be traced?"

"Sure. If it's legitimately registered. I'll get somebody on it. We're looking into the Tom Kingston boats right now."

"Who is he anyway?"

"Kingston? I'll ask." He bit my ear and kissed my cheek. "Got to run. I'll be around for part of the opening. Tony will have some people in plain clothes, too."

"I'm expecting Pasquin and Mama to show up at any moment."

I walked to the edge of the river, doing my best to avoid stepping in mud puddles. The fury of the currents had subsided for now and the water lay in a calm mist that rose from the water half way up the banks. A couple of late starting fishermen moved slowly from the river to the bay. They seemed sleepy, their hearts not into fighting with big fish on strong hooks today. They nodded as they passed me.

"Lovely time of day, isn't it?"

I turned to see O'Neil approaching me. He had a coffee mug in his hand and sipped it loud enough to disturb the forest silence.

"The best time, other than black night with a full moon," I said.

"Not for me. Things happen in the night. That's when predatory animals feed on helpless things. Of course, those helpless things are feeding on other helpless things. The food chain is too active at night." He sighed. "No. This is the time of day for me."

"And Sheila? Does she love it, too?"

O'Neil frowned. "She used to. Always got up at dawn and

wandered outside." He shook his head. "Not anymore. Says mornings aren't her time now."

I felt he didn't want to talk about her, that something sad had sneaked its way into their lives.

"I see your neighbor hasn't rented any of her tubes."

O'Neil turned to look back at the array of trailers. "You mean the Gibson woman? No. Who's going to run down this river with those currents?"

"You'd be surprised at what teenagers will do," I said.

"Haven't seen any about. Just two younger boys with their grandpa."

I nodded and wondered if those kids had any better luck on the river with their hooks and worms.

"You're going to the opening?"

"Oh, wouldn't miss it," said O'Neil. "I have to take Sheila a covered dish. She says it won't do for a reader to show up in such a public place. She's going to eat in the shop."

It sounded strange to me, but I reckoned a reader was a strange human specimen anyway. Marci would have to burn extra incense to cover the odor of fried fish and hushpuppies.

Pasquin told me he'd deliver Mama to the new dock where we'd landed the first time he brought us here. I had to pick her up and drive the short distance to the café.

The shop and café areas were bursting with activity when I drove by on my way to the dock. Balloons floated above each corner of the café. I heard something like a Cajun fiddle coming from the speaker system. Two young men were setting up small round tables with chairs outside the front of the café. If anyone planned to eat out there at noon, they'd roast and be sunburned in a matter of minutes.

Mama came dressed in her white uniform. She carried an apron she would put around her ample waist when it was time. I helped her lift a cooler from Pasquin's boat.

"Careful with that. It's got some nice hushpuppy dough already to be tossed into the oil."

"Kayleen doesn't make her own?"

"Probably does, but just a little way I can help out. She's using my recipe anyway." Mama gave the boat a dirty look and turned to my car. "Oh, yes, another little dinky thing to ride in."

"My boat isn't dinky," said Pasquin and slapped his hat against his leg.

"It is if you're my size." She stared inside the Honda. When she finally wedged herself into the passenger seat and Pasquin had slipped into the back, we headed for the café.

"Crazy things have been happening here," I said.

"We heard," said Pasquin. "Gibby broke Bub's arm."

"I guess he'll be no help today," said Mama.

"According to Kayleen, he wasn't much help anyway." I turned into the parking lot and pulled around to the back door of the café. The two young men were loading empty boxes into the dumpster.

"Is everything ready?" I asked.

"Just about. Kayleen's cooking up a storm. Don't cross her."

The other one looked up at the outdoor speaker. "Guess we'll have to listen to that stuff all day and night."

"Nice fiddler," said Pasquin and tapped the guy on his shoulder with his hat brim. "I think she'll change to some zydeco later on, maybe even a country-western or two."

"Not many customers are going to go for that rap stuff," said Mama. "Not even that other loud rock stuff."

The two had been chastised and made eyes at each other. They returned to trashing the boxes.

The kitchen bustled with pots of grits boiling on the stove, batter being prepared for the fish, and cabbage being grated for a mountain of slaw. On the other side, a table had been set aside for preparing the Cajun style food. A mass of red crawfish sat in a large pan. One woman was chopping the ingredients for gumbo.

"It's all too dizzying for me," I said. "I manage a microwave."

"Then go on out," said Mama. "I got a cell phone, and I know how to use it. I'll let you know when you're needed." She made it clear that Pasquin and I were not to be underfoot, and I was most happy not to be. We left in a hurry, driving to the front of the shops.

"Let's visit old Harold," said Pasquin.

Harold knew his bread might gather more butter today and he dressed for the occasion. He stuck a bow tie onto a clean blue shirt.

"I even swept inside the shop," he said. "Stuck up some corner lights so all the junk can be seen."

"You mean there is something worth buying back in that corner?" Pasquin laughed and pointed to a pile of unidentifiable iron at the far end.

"Some folks find valuables in here." Harold winked at me. "You folks want some coffee?"

Pasquin nodded, and the two men took seats Harold had placed just outside his front door. I waved off the brew and decided to visit the Talisman.

Marci's balloons were different. Instead of the red, white and blue of Harold's Oddities and Mo's Convenience Store, these were shades of light and dark blue with whisps of white. It lended an ethereal suggestion to match the door sprite and Marci's scarf top. She wore a scarf skirt today, one that draped in an uneven hem around her knees. The whole outfit gave the appearance of material merely draped about her body.

I stopped to read a sign in the window. It had been carefully designed to attract the eye with faded images of eyes staring from a foggy mist.

READINGS BY SHEILA
APPOINTMENT NECESSARY.

Inside, Sheila sat on a chair in the back and fanned herself. Marci stood over her with a glass of water.

"Is everything okay?" I asked as I approached the two women.

Sheila nodded, her face in a terrible sweat. "I just hurried too much this morning. I keep forgetting I'm not a native to this humidity." She took a sip of the water and nodded toward Marci.

Miss Doucet turned slowly toward me, a smile on her face, but her eyes half closed. I was reminded of being noticed by a cobra.

"She has so much business she can barely handle it all." The words came softly through the incensed air.

"People heard about the Cardel incident," I said. "Getting it right must be part of the attraction."

Marci frowned. "The cards are never wrong," she said. "It's just the interpretation is not always correct."

"Haven't missed one yet," said Sheila. She leaned back in the chair and closed her eyes. "This heat spell is passing."

"Will your brother be in to help today?" I watched Marci's expression. Did she know anything about the liason with Kayleen?

"Perhaps. But he has to be on the Gulf soon. Shrimp don't come to you." She took the glass from Sheila and headed to a small bathroom in the back. "I'll be here all day. Can't afford to leave the shop in anyone's hands."

"No, I guess you can't. Takes someone with a different kind of knowledge to sell this stuff." I turned to Sheila. "Are you booked up today?"

"Yes. Solid. I think I'd best meditate a little before I start." She pushed herself up from the chair and nearly staggered to her little reading room. Instead of closing the door behind her, I watched her dig into a purse on the table and pull out a bottle of pills. She reached one hand around and slammed shut the door.

"Will her husband check on her today?" I asked Marci as she returned to the main room of the shop.

"Why do you ask that?" It was a genuine question, one with some shock, I thought.

"She says she's booked solid. I'd think she'd need a break and maybe some food."

Marci placed a hand on her chest in the manner of a Victorian woman's near fainting spell. "Well, yes, he'll help out in that way." She stared at me as though not knowing what else to say.

I turned to look around the store. All the bins and racks had been replenished. "I'll run on now. Good luck to you today."

Marci smiled and nodded, still silent.

Mo sat behind his counter and gave a half wave when I entered.

"I've done a year's business already," he said. "These fishermen went out earlier than usual so they can come back to the café gala. It's just fish and grits, for heaven's sake!"

"You'll do more business when they return," I said. "By the way, how well do you know the shrimp boats and their owners?"

"Some fairly well. Others not at all. Depends on whether or not they stay at Crusty Dock, go on up the river, or stop by the camp. That one's brother comes in now and then." He darted his thumb toward Marci's shop.

"His boat is named The Talisman, I understand."

"Yep. Guess they both believe in magic doing a number on your life. Not here. Hard work is all there is. Wish I could say 'poof!' and money would appear in the register."

"Is the brother anything like his sister? I mean kind of gentle natured?"

"Hummpf! He's what I'd call a lothario." He stretched the word into its syllables. "I learned that a long time ago in a high school English class. Been a useful word around fishermen."

I laughed. "Why do you say that?"

Mo lifted his slight body half way across the counter and said as though someone could be listening in the empty shop, "He's got quite a list of ladies, you know. And guess who is one of them?"

I shook my head.

"Little miss new café owner," he said. "Been caught in the flesh so I hear."

I smiled. The word was out, then, and I had no idea how. Of course, Mo could have been nearby when we discovered the two. His radar would be as good as any swamp rat's.

"And what does his sister think of this lady thing?"

"Don't like it much. My trailer ain't far from hers and boy does she give it to him some nights when he comes in late."

I laughed again. "I had no idea she could raise her voice at all."

"Don't let that act fool you. She's got the shrew down pat, that one has."

"With his job on the Gulf, I'd think Bernard wouldn't have time or opportunity to have his liasons too often."

"Don't kid yourself. He comes in almost every night. I don't know how much business that boat does, but he seems to stay ashore a lot."

Mo sat back in his chair with a beer he had grabbed from a

cooler behind the counter. I figured the conversation had ended. All I needed to do now was head back to see if Harold knew all the dirt.

He did. As soon as I asked if he knew Bernard Doucet very well, he laughed. "Why? He been putting the amore bird on you, too?"

"Not hardly." I sat on the ground near the chair. Pasquin stared at me from under his hat, his eyes squinting as though asking *what are you up to, woman?*

"He's got a feeling or two about yon Kayleen," said Harold who pointed toward the café. "Imagine he'll bring in his entire crew for a meal tonight. Might even stay and help out afterwards. Old Bub ain't worth a damn with a broken arm."

"I don't suppose Bernard brings other women around here?"

"Hadn't exactly seen any, just heard he's got the itch."

Pasquin and Harold laughed out loud. "Been more than fifty years since I got that itch!" said Pasquin, and Harold nodded in agreement.

I left the two old men to nod off, wake up and joke some more, then nod off again. Grand openings were just more days in the routine to them.

Two women wearing Bermuda shorts, which revealed un-sightly varicose veins, entered the Talisman as I passed the door. I overheard them whispering about what they might find out, and I assumed they were headed for a reading. "Wonder if they are hoping their husbands will be found dead," I said to myself and the wind.

The wonderful fragrance of frying fish came from Kayleen's Café. People from the fish camp, the boats, and surrounding towns began to park in the lot and wander about the area. Two fat men with sunburns and suspenders holding up their shorts headed toward Harold's Oddities. Pasquin would have to clean up his act a little.

Kayleen had installed a fan over the doorway to try and blow out any unwanted flies. The air blew out the smells, too, and stomachs were growling. She wouldn't open until noon, but a line was forming.

I stood to the side and watched people gather from nowhere, it seemed. Most were from inland areas, including Tallahassee. The lot was nearly full when a van pulled into two spaces. It had the local television station logo on the outside.

"You're covering a café opening?" I said to the young woman who was heavily made up for the camera. She wore a sundress that showed off well tanned shoulders.

"Not just a café opening," she said. "This one is right in the middle of a crime scene."

CHAPTER SEVENTEEN

What better way to attract customers than to let them gawk at the place where bodies had been found? It would work for Kayleen today, and I wondered if she'd been read by Sheila after all.

Tony kept his word and turned out several deputies for the occasion. A couple were conspicuous in uniforms, but the others wore beach clothing and blended in with tourists and fishermen alike. Vernon wasn't scheduled to appear until later, closer to supper time.

I wandered toward Harold's place. Ladies with short haircuts dragged their husbands through the iron and wood junk, pointing out relics they wanted for a den or a boat. The husbands shelled out cash, giving Harold whole half hours on his feet. Pasquin roamed the room, pretending to look but actually keeping an eye out for shoplifters. "Junk is something even honest people have no qualms about taking," he said.

I stood in the narrow shade of the overhang outside and smiled at the constant flow of people. Kayleen still hadn't opened, but a line formed at the door. It would be a long hot wait for late comers.

A lady with a Brooklyn accent came to the door and peeped inside Harold's. "Somebody said he might have an old anchor here." She looked directly at me.

"He could have. Not sure if I'd use it at sea, but it would

make a nice decoration."

"Oh, yes. That's what I want it for, my den. Does he have a ship's wheel, too?"

I shrugged. "I don't work here."

She stepped inside. Behind her, the tall Bernard Doucet gave me a smile and a wink. "I'm on a mission," he said. "Kayleen needs two sturdy tables to hold up a long board. She has run out of room to prepare the crawfish."

I looked at him for a moment. His eyes twinkled with boyish guilt, and a smile kept twitching on one side of his mouth. Fulfilling Kayleen's needs was only one of his talents.

"Does she have a board?"

"Yes, there's an old cutting board about the size of a long table. They're cleaning it off now, but they need props."

I waved my hand toward the entrance. "He's got some iron frames for tables," I said.

I turned and watched Bernard search hurriedly through the mishmash of junk. He was probably taller than Vernon, slim but solid, like someone who worked out. His dark hair and blue eyes were set off by the even tan. More years on the ocean and he'd look like leather with lots of gray in that thick curly hair, but for now, he seemed almost Latino.

Bernard found his two tables, paid for them, and left carrying one in each hand.

I drifted next door. Getting inside the Talisman was nearly impossible now. People gathered around the amulet boxes and touched the blessed necklaces on the wall. They flipped through books and smelled soap. Some couldn't deal with the heavy incense and left fanning the air in front of their noses. A line had formed outside Sheila's closed door. It had nowhere to go and kept moving around to allow shoppers to see the merchandise.

Chaos had entered the scarf queen's abode, and she flitted about like a drunken butterfly. I watched her slight body, small boned, extremely fair skin, and reddish blond hair. Blue eyes sat in delicate face, perhaps Irish in ancestry. "No Latina here," I said.

"Look at this trash," said Marci who shoved a handful of flyers into a trash can behind her counter. "Everybody has taken the café opening as their time and place to advertise."

Not to mention the Talisman, I wanted to say. A couple of flyers dropped from the overly full can onto the floor. When she wasn't looking, I picked them up and read the ads, mostly made on a computer and copied in mass quantities.

One was a familiar boat yard that rented small craft to tourists and got them a temporary boat license if they needed it. Kayaks and canoes were also in the offering. The other was a shell craft shop where they not only sold every imaginable shell off a sea creature but also taught you how to make jewelry from them. I dropped them back into the can and gave my own talisman a touch, the holy shrimp that was hanging around my neck and down my shirt.

The crowd was stifling, and I headed away from those who would believe in trinkets that would heal. It was Saturday. Tomorrow, they would all go to their various churches and swear that only God could heal. I was willing to bet Saturdays were a lot more fun.

"Anything of interest around here?" A familiar voice sounded from my right shoulder as I backed away from the shop. "Or are we paying for trailer space just to give you a vacation."

"Why, Tony! Imagine you at a party on the coast." I turned to take a tall plastic glass of iced tea from him. He had one of his own that had condensed and was dripping on his khaki shorts. He had tried his best to be informal. His tee shirt was a bit too new, and the flipflops weren't going to do him any service if he had to chase someone. He wore his aviator sun glasses. But the thick head of black hair was still slicked back and combed. Whatever he used on it, it wasn't going to blow in the gentle breezes.

I took in the whole sight. "Well, I'll be," I said.

"Don't get smart," he said. "I asked you a question."

"Yeah. I need a favor." I turned away and looked toward the café. "Of course, Vernon could do it, but he's not standing here right now."

"What?"

"Bernard Doucet. Vernon had some sketchy info on him. I'd like more, including a photo if possible."

"Why?"

"Have you seen Marci?" I nodded toward the Talisman. "Bernard is her brother. No word on whether he's a half or adopted brother—which might explain things. But in that info, there was something about being an amateur bantam weight fighter at one time in his life."

"Explain what?"

"He and his sister look like they're from two entirely different sets of genes. Dark and light. Tall and short. Big boned and tiny boned. If you'll walk around behind the café with me, I can show you Bernard in the flesh."

"Maybe I should see the sister first."

I nodded toward the shop. "Go on in. Meet me behind the café."

The back of the café was nearly as busy as the front. A delivery truck from Crusty Dock had backed up to the rigged table. Bernard and another worker held some large tubs, half filled with ice, while the unloaders dumped in crawfish and crab. The table, merely the two iron frames beneath what looked like a dining table top board, held both tubs, one at each end. I watched until the truck started to pull away. It moved slowly onto the bay road and shifted gears on its way back to the dock.

"Okay. She's small and light," said Tony, who again came up from the right.

"Look at the guy icing up the crawfish," I said and nodded toward Bernard. "He's the one we caught with the owner the other night. Surely, you heard about it."

"Haven't heard much else." He lowered his head and raised his eyes to stare at Bernard. "Tall, dark, and..." He turned his face away.

"Handsome, yes. But does he look like his sister? Or even a bantam weight boxer?"

"Nope." Tony looked back at Bernard. The two of them could have been brothers, or maybe father and son. Tony was tall, dark, and most thought rather handsome. Of course, no one would ever catch him in the nude with some married café owner.

"Can your computer files find anything else on him?"

"We'll try," he said.

"Then there is the matter of Zeke Owen, the rather strange little PI."

"Oh, him." Tony smiled. "He came looking for the Guerrin woman, didn't find her, so he played a few days in the Gulf. Went fishing with one of the higher class excursion boats. He's back in Louisiana now."

I nodded. The mistrust of private detectives would have meant a strict tail on the man. I figured Marci was glad to see him leave, too.

A surge of lunchers crowded under the fan at the restaurant door. It could have been the opening of some grand restaurant in New York, only the clientele wore shorts and sandals instead of designer gowns. I didn't even want to think about Mama and the amount of work she'd volunteered for in that kitchen.

"Are you going to eat?" I asked.

"I'll wait for the evening meal. Maybe most of the beach crowd will be gone."

There was no possibility of getting through that line. I started walking toward the camp, away from the crowds. Others were doing the same, even people who didn't live there. They wouldn't go as far as I would. Children romped about the palmettos until they realized they were out of touch with the crowd.

When I reached the clearing, I stopped. Gibby was standing there, talking to Bub. He had broken the man's arm and been kicked out of his wife's trailer and now here he was, shaking Bub's good hand and pulling up a chair next to him.

"Are you better today?" I asked Bub, really wanting to know about Gibby.

"Yeah. Me and Gibby made it up. Not much to do but sit here and soak up—the sun?" He lifted a bottle from beneath his chair and took a swig. He passed it to Gibby, who briefly looked guilty. The pull of alcohol, however, was too strong and he became Bub's afternoon drinking partner.

"Are you moving back in with Carol?" I asked Gibby.

He shrugged, his pitiful eyes darting back and forth from me to Bub. "If she'll have me."

She won't, I said to myself. I had seen the determination on her face and the boxes of Gibby's personal stuff floating in the rain. This was one determined woman.

I bid them a good afternoon and walked toward my trailer. There was no sign of Plato. He hadn't been at the opening, either. He didn't bother with big groups of people, preferring to romp about the forest.

I pulled out some of the leftovers from Mama's Table and heated a lunch for myself. It wouldn't be crab claws or gumbo, but there wouldn't be a line, either. With a few hush puppies in hand, I stood at the front and gazed out my door. Bub and Gibby passed the bottle back and forth until Gibby tipped it over and realized it was empty. He tried to stand and sat back down hard on the beach chair. Both men laughed hard. Bub took his good hand and rummaged through his shirt pocket and pulled out some bills. He handed them over to Gibby. It would be a trip to Mo's for another bottle, but for a staggering Gibby, he might never arrive. Somewhere along this mission he realized that and pointed to the tubes in front of the trailer. The sign to rent them was still there but it was tilted to one side. No one could see what it said.

Gibby grabbed one tube with both arms and dragged it to Bub. He returned and got the second one for himself. Bub struggled to stand, his arm in a cast that gave him little freedom on that side. With his good arm, he dragged the inner tube toward the river bank. Gibby followed, staggering and losing the tube several times.

At first, I thought they were just going to sit on the tubes atop the bank. Two drunks communing with nature. I should have known better. When they reached the top, they shoved the tubes, making them come to rest right at the water's edge.

"Oh, my God!" I said. I raced from the trailer, dropping hush puppies for the sea gulls. "Hey! Don't go into the water with those." It was too late. Both men had flopped backward onto the tubes and pushed off with their feet. Bub had given a sharp cry when he hit his, but his pain must have been numbed by the drink. He started laughing along with Gibby.

The tide was in, a dangerous time for anyone tubing this river. Things were soon out of hand as the tubes began to swirl and then move off through the swift running water. I ran for the cell phone and the canoe. What I could do from that position, I had no idea. Saving one man in these currents would be tough. I made a quick call to Tony and let him know to get out the emergency boats.

The canoe proved a hard paddle in the swift water. I tried to keep behind the two men instead of taking a more peaceful path. They raced ahead of me, both whooping and hollering like teenagers on their first run. Bub held his cast arm above like a beacon, his barefeet sticking up at the other end. Gibby began to circle as well as move rapidly away from his friend. His whooping stopped, and I could see his facial expression change to fright. It wasn't fright of the water but of the liquor that was now making him sick. He tried leaning over but the swirling pushed him back. Vomit flew into nature and disappeared into the river. He finally leaned back, his arms outstretched in crucifixion form on top of the inner tube.

I wasn't going to be able to pull them out of the water. Instead, I followed them, ready to rescue one if he fell overboard. The tubes circled and raced toward some overhanging oak limbs.

"Keep your heads down!" I yelled. If one raised up, he could be slapped right off by a heavy limb. Worse, if a moccasin rested on a limb, it could fall onto the tube with him. It had happened to people in boats.

When I heard a boat siren coming from the other direction, I breathed a sigh of relief and slowed the canoe. The tubes had caught on limbs beneath the trees and didn't come out the other side. Bub kept yelling to come untangle him. Gibby was quiet, most likely gagging by now since he'd emptied whatever was on his stomach.

The rescue boat moved close to the trees and pulled the tubes toward it. Instead of taking the men on board, they towed them to shore. Neither could pull himself up and waited for the deputies to come off the boat and fix them to a sitting position on the bank. I waved at them from my side of trees and turned the canoe back toward the camp.

Both Tony and Vernon were at the camp when I pulled ashore. Vernon helped me take the canoe to its resting place.

"That Gibson woman isn't going to like this, but she's going to have to give up her rental business," said Vernon.

"I don't think Bub and Gibby paid any rent."

"She's got them out in the open by her sign and no one around to see that they aren't taken. Plus, she's got no safety rules or instructions. All she needs is for some kid to drown in the currents."

"Not to mention a much disliked husband."

"Or a would-be savior in a canoe," Vernon laughed now. "But you've got your holy shrimp to protect you."

Tony left an official warning on Carol Gibson's door. She'd have to earn her extra money in tips now. Before we headed back to the café, O'Neil's car pulled up next to his trailer.

"He's got Sheila with him," I said. "I wonder if she finished all those people's readings."

"Looks more like she needs a break," said Vernon.

O'Neil went to the passenger side and helped his wife to her feet. She staggered a bit, her face looking much like Gibby's on the swirling tube.

"Is everything okay?" I asked as I approached to help open the trailer door.

"Oh, yes. She just got overly tired and didn't eat. I called a halt to it all. Just hold the door while I get her inside." Sheila rested on her husband's shoulder, closing her eyes off and on as though in great pain. She had no color.

O'Neil closed the door as I stood at the threshold. "Let me know if you need anything," I shouted.

A muffled, "I will," came back to me.

Tony was on the phone with the rescue deputies.

"Both men are being checked out at the Palmetto Springs Clinic," he said. "Most likely the worse thing will be drunkeness."

Vernon looked at both of us. "Shall we try for a big fish dinner at Kayleen's Café? I hear the zydeco music is going full blast."

CHAPTER EIGHTEEN

Not only was the zydeco music going full blast over the sound system, a few old codgers had pulled up crates outside the café and were making their own rhythms. They either sang along with the CD or grunted out beats with melodic voices. From their dress, I knew they were off the boats, crewmen who had handled shrimp and salt water for days.

"You better take a table while you can," said Mama. She met us as we entered the café. The air conditioning worked its best but too many door openings defeated it. The odors of frying fish did their best to pass through the vents.

"Pasquin and his buddy are over there." Mama pointed to a table where Harold had joined Pasquin. They were picking through a huge platter of crawfish.

"We'll sit here and watch you take care of that," said Vernon. "Pretty hot stuff, huh?"

"Just right," said Pasquin. His companion smiled, a piece of red crawfish shell sticking from his broken teeth.

We ate then, mostly Southern seafood platters. The Cajun stuff burned like Vernon said. We did top it all off with beignets, warm sweet donut treats, a sort of Louisiana cousin to Mexican churros.

"So two old swampers went for a ride on inner tubes," said Pasquin. He laughed and shook his head. "Got to be good and drunk to do that with a broken arm."

169

"And they were good and drunk," I said. "If Carol despised her husband before, she'll be ready to drown him after this."

I looked across the room. Carol was busy carrying a large round tray full of crab platters. The table she served had three young kids who turned up their noses and showed amazement at the same time. When one of the men showed them how to pull out the meat from the crab leg, they decided to enjoy them with butter.

"Sell much junk today?" asked Vernon.

Harold grinned. "You'd be surprised just what people will buy when it's all together in a shop called Oddities. They think they're getting something."

"Who's minding the store right now?" I asked. There were still people wandering about the walk in front of the shops.

"Nobody. I put the CLOSED sign on the door and walked away. Belly was growling."

"Not just everybody is chasing big bucks, you know," said Pasquin.

By the time we finished, darkness had nearly settled over the bay café and shops. Kayleen had turned on the lights that outlined her place. It would be a beacon from a ship way out in the bay.

"I need some rest for these old legs," said Mama as she joined us, setting a plate of fish and grits on the table for herself. "Got my special way if anybody wants to come to the shore with me later on."

We all looked at each other. Mama never went near the water as far as we knew. She hated riding in boats that she felt might tip her into the river.

"I'll go," I said.

"Me too" echoed around the table.

"Now, look. This ain't for spectacle. I do it to cure sore

muscles." She raised a filet to her mouth and took a bite off it. "Kayleen does a mighty good job on her cooking."

We all agreed. The café still had some customers who sat chatting over coffee, some of it from the espresso maker.

Vernon and I agreed to see each other later. The men decided against watching Mama ease her legs, leaving it to me to escort her.

She grabbed a bath towel from the large bag she had brought to the opening and headed down the shore, away from the crowds. I followed until she came to an area where gentle water washed onto clean white sand. She tossed the towel on the sand just where the water couldn't reach it, and with great grunting difficulty sat down, her chubby legs outstretched. I hadn't noticed, but she wore no shoes. With more effort she wiggled her behind closer to the edge of the water just so the waves would wash over her thighs but no higher. It was a precision I'd never seen before.

"It's the water, you see. Salty and just a little warm." She leaned back on her hands and looked at the stars. "Better than a bathtub any day."

I sat a ways back from her, taking off my shoes and soaking only my feet. "You don't do this at your own place, do you?"

She looked over at me, her round cheeks in a grin. "You'd be surprised what I do, Miss Luanne."

"But the water is cold there."

"Yes. It is. But I got this spot out back. I sit on a chair and stick my legs into a tub of warm water. Takes the kinks out." She laughed quietly. "Bet you didn't know I had a hot water tap put in back there just for that reason."

I didn't know a lot, it seemed, about people I'd known for years.

We sat like that for nearly an hour, talking about the clear skies and how fate pushes people onto shores they never thought they'd see.

"I wonder what it's like to sleep all night on a shrimp boat," I said. In the distance, I saw the rigging lights of one coming to shore.

"Couldn't be all that comfortable," Mama said. "It gets rough sometimes, and I don't mean the ocean. I've seen men come in with infections where they cut themselves on some of that rigging. They don't doctor it right away and get some bad fevers with it."

We let more silence fall between us again. The idea of fever brought the image of Sheila's face to my head.

"You know, Mrs. O'Neil, Sheila the Reader, sure looked bad tonight. Her husband brought her to their trailer and nearly had to carry her inside. She looked kind of green."

Mama spoke without opening her eyes. "That woman is ill. I've seen it too many times in my life. She's got something more than hocus-pocus talent."

"You think?"

"Bet you a piece of key lime pie on it."

I helped Mama up, not an easy task with her weight and her totally relaxed body. She walked barefoot back to the café.

"Carol will take me home," she said. "They should be about cleaned up by now."

"You don't plan to return tomorrow?" I asked.

"Oh, no. I need to tend to my own place. Hope those assistants didn't ruin anything while I was gone." She looked around the parking area. "Where's Carol's vehicle?"

Kayleen came outside and stretched her back. Bernard Doucet followed and massaged her shoulders. I had the feeling he was going to pull her close and kiss her neck until he spied us.

"Oh, Carol said to tell you she had to run. Seems Gibby got himself in more trouble. He's at the Palmetto Springs Clinic."

"Along with your husband," I said. "Is she going to check on him, too?"

"He's all right. Carol said she'd bring them both home. Gibby cut his foot on something when he got off the tube." She sounded disgusted. "Two idiots, two blights on an otherwise quite successful day."

I turned to Mama. "I'll drive you home. I need to check on my house anyway. Pasquin has been going there to make sure no bear has taken up residence."

Mama nodded. "More like a flock of green lizards." She was staring at Bernard who had backed away and leaned against the wall of the café.

Mama tossed her bag of personal goods into the back of the Honda and relaxed in the passenger seat. She rested her head on the door, and I was afraid she'd be sound asleep by the time we got to the Fogarty Spring landing.

"That woman is in for trouble if she gets involved with that Doucet man," she said suddenly.

"She is involved with him," I said, without telling the tale of discovery in the storage room. "It's pretty obvious."

"Fiddling with him, maybe. That's one thing, but involved is all about the place and the money. He's not somebody I'd trust."

Fiddling meant anything from sex to more sex and it signified nothing to many people. As long as it stayed in the storeroom and away from kids' eyes, it was nobody's business. But when fiddling neared the pocket book, look out!

"She wouldn't be such a fool, would she?"

"Kayleen likes loving," said Mama. "Bub ain't given her anything but a barber's rash and second hand smoke for years." She shifted her head for a more comfortable position on the neck rest. "Be better off if she'd let him float away in Katrina."

I laughed without saying anything. Mama didn't like Bub. That was clear.

"Bub didn't help with a thing. Not even before he broke that arm," said Mama. "He tried to get her to take down the ad on their trailer and said she was spending too much on those hand-out papers. Too bad he couldn't see the customers she got to-day."

We rode in silence the rest of the way to her place. Mama had her own husband who wasn't allowed around anymore. She said they just cost too much. With Kayleen's success at her restaurant and her flesh comforts from Bernard, what would she need with Bub at all?

A sleepy Mama waved her goodbyes and drifted into her little house in Fogarty Spring. Her bundle nearly dragged behind her. I knew she'd be up to make breakfast for early fishermen tomor-row morning. This was her life, one she played out on her own terms.

I turned toward my own house but changed my mind and sped on back to the little trailer and Vernon, I hoped. If I went to my house now, I might want to stay the night.

Vernon was already in bed when I got there. Plato had ap-peared and slept on his pillow on the floor. He wagged his tail a few times and nodded off again. I crawled into the other bed, brushing the beach sand off my feet. Maybe with Gibby's foot bandaged, we wouldn't be awakened by a ruckus tonight. I sud-denly felt the weariness come over me and slept until sunlight came through the tiny window in the kitchen.

Plato whined to be let out, and I rose to see Vernon's bed empty. The shower was going and the coffee pot spewed and sputtered out its welcome brew.

I sat on a dining chair in my night shirt and sipped the strong stuff. Watching Plato sniff out all the trailers amused me, like he had to make sure they passed his inspection before he let them stay.

Vernon dressed himself quietly. Neither of us liked early morning noises. The silence of calm at this hour was better than therapy. It didn't last.

An ambulance siren blasted through the trees. Plato jumped and came running. He wouldn't come in but stayed protectively on the front steps. He began to howl as his ears ached with the approaching siren.

"It's coming here," I said.

Vernon was on the phone, asking what the emergency was and if he'd have to be part of it.

Before he could report what he'd been told, the ambulance hit the clearing and moved slowly around to the O'Neil trailer. Mr. O'Neil stood in his doorway, waving to the driver.

"It's Sheila," I said. "Mama said she was ill."

The EMTs spent what seemed an eternity inside the little trailer. When they finally emerged with the stretcher, Sheila lay on it, her eyes closed but her head turning side to side.

Vernon joined the ambulance and spoke to one of the paramedics. When they lifted Sheila into the back, they urged her husband to ride with them. He shook his head, his face white and full of fear.

Vernon finally motioned to me that he'd follow the ambulance with O'Neil just to get the guy to accompany his wife.

I sat down and listened to the shrill fade away into the distance as the ambulance made its way to a clinic or maybe a hospital in Tallahassee. Outside, a small group had gathered only to stand in bewilderment. Could the reader not read her own future? Maybe she had.

I dressed and walked toward the shops. Plato followed along and checked out the entire way. As soon as we came to the edge of the complex, he took off for Harold's Oddities.

"Okay, you little bum dog. Be careful or you'll be sold for junk."

I stood in front of the Talisman. Inside, Marci combed her long hair in front of a mirror framed with astrological signs. She spoke, too, and at first I thought she was talking to herself. When she turned abruptly and screamed "NO!" loud enough for me to hear outside, I realized someone else was there.

Her brother made an appearance behind her. He took her hair and wrapped it around his palm. The process slowly pulled her head back. He looked into her upturned eyes and said something with a fierceness I hadn't thought him capable of feeling. She turned, saw me outside and mouthed something. He let go.

Inside, I pretended not to have noticed.

"We just opened. You're early," said Marci, her breathiness taking on a bit of anxiousness.

"I came to ask if you knew what happened to Sheila. The ambulance took her away this morning."

Both Marci and Bernard stood very still. They stared at me until Marci found her voice. "That was Sheila? I heard it but I was sure it would be one of those drunken idiots. Kayleen's husband, maybe." She half turned toward her brother.

"What is wrong with Sheila?" I asked.

Marci moved to her stool behind the counter. Bernard stayed in the same spot and watched her.

"She's a cancer patient," said Marci. "Has had recurrances and been through chemo. I think this last time, they told her it was terminal. She decided not to do the chemo anymore and to just let it go." Marci's eyes watered a bit as she looked toward the sign over the reading room. "She wanted this job to make a little extra money. They had just about depleted everything over the years of treatments."

"You knew this when she asked for a job?"

"Oh, no. I advertised for the job. She fit the bill. I made a little off the rental of the room. She earned some from readings. She helped attract customers to the store."

"Especially when word got out that she could really predict catastrophe."

Marci nodded. Her brother still watched her.

"That Cardel woman is a talker. She brought in a lot of extra money."

"If she is terminal," I said. "What will her husband do?"

"He's devoted to her. He won't last long."

We both turned when the sprite over the door jingled her bell. Two men, obviously sailors from one of the boats, came in and stood before Marci.

"You got any idea where Bernard is?" said one. "He's supposed to go out with us today and we've been holding the boat for him."

I turned to the spot where Bernard had eyed his sister. He was gone, vanished like one of the spirits in the paint.

"We're going to have to leave without him," said the other man. "We've already missed good hours."

Marci stared at the men.

"I'll tell him if I see him," she whispered.

I shrugged when she looked at me, and made a mental note to call Marshall about some bookends.

CHAPTER NINETEEN

If her brother was shacked up with Kayleen, Marci was going to fry him. Her eyes, cold and bitter, followed the men as they left the shop. She sighed as soon as they were out of sight. As though she had forgotten I was there, she looked up and smiled one of her phony smiles.

"Poor Sheila." She glanced back at the room. "I've done readings in my time, but I can't stop to do them now. I'll have to look for someone else."

"Are there many of these readers around?"

"Tarot card readers, yes. Some are better than others. I'll have to try some out, I guess."

"Maybe a series of guest readers, if you can find that many."

Her eyes smiled along with her lips this time. "Oh, you just came up with the best idea. I'm going to try that." She moved to the reading room and pointed to Sheila's sign. "I'll change that to THE READING ROOM and put one of those portable name holders here." She measured a place on the side wall with her hands. "It will announce the name of the reader for the day." On her way back to the counter, she touched my arm. "You are the clever one."

I nodded, not knowing how to accept praise from someone I considered a fake, and left the shop.

Walking past Harold's, I saw he was sound asleep in a chair at his front door. Rather than disturb him, I moved on to Mo's. He was behind his counter, reading the local paper.

"Do you carry crossword puzzle books here?" I asked, just to get conversation started. I glanced over his news rack.

He put down his paper. "Sounds like you're getting bored with this little vacation. Try the bottom. Should be all kinds of puzzle books there. You'd be surprised how many women spend time with them. Their husbands rush off to sit on a boat, hold a pole in the water, and drink their weight in beer." He shrugged. "Of course, I'm not complaining as long as they buy the beer and the puzzles from me."

"I guess you heard Sheila O'Neil is in the hospital."

"Somebody told me the ambulance took her off this morning. I get here so early I miss anything that happens later than dawn. What's the matter with her?"

"Marci Doucet says it's cancer."

Mo shook his head. "Bad stuff. Took my own mother." He stopped talking and went back to his paper.

I bought a crossword puzzle book, and to look authentic, a pencil and sharpener combo. Wandering once more along the road to the trailer camp, I waited to hear from Vernon. I didn't wait long.

"She died?" I stopped in my tracks. "So quickly?"

"Not quickly, evidently," said Vernon over his cell phone. "She'd been dying for months. Took a turn for the worse and couldn't breathe last night. That's why her husband called the ambulance, but he knew what the result would be."

"And how is he doing now?" I envisioned the stocky man sitting in his beach chair, sipping a soda, and talking to me.

"That's why I called. He didn't want to ride in the ambulance with her. He said he didn't want to watch her die. I dropped him in the emergency room and turned him over to the nurse there. Seems he disappeared after that. People at the hospital haven't been able to find him anywhere. I wondered if he'd gone back to his trailer."

I promised to check and hurried toward the camp. Things seemed normal there. It may be Sunday, but fishermen no longer went by the old Puritan rule of no fishing on the holy day. Most were gone before the ambulance came.

I knocked on the O'Neil door. No one answered. Turning the knob, I found it had not been locked when they left in such a hurry. Inside, the tiny place was a mess, most likely turned upside down by the EMTs who took Sheila out on a stretcher. The trailer wasn't too much larger than the one I stayed in, but it had some medical equipment behind one of the beds. Someone had rigged a holder for an oxygen tank, the kind with nasal tubes. It sat there, its tubes coiled and waiting to guide oxygen into a living person. A shelf held a multitude of pill bottles. There was a blanket on one bed, and the air conditioning was off, making the atmosphere inside the small space feel stale and humid. "She would get cold," I said to myself. "I'll bet they didn't turn it on often." It must have been a nightly reminder to O'Neil that his wife was dying. A stocky man like him would get hot at night. Outside would be no better unless there was a rare breeze off the bay.

I jumped when my phone rang.

"Luanne," said Vernon. "It seems the man paid a big sum for a taxi to take him to the boat rental just upriver from the camp. I called the place. He rented a small motor boat and took off right there. He's somewhere in the area."

Vernon said they were having to call a rescue boat from another job, but I could move about in the canoe, with a promise that I'd call if I found anything. He didn't say it, but I knew they meant suicide.

"You'd best notify the Coast Guard in case he went out into the bay, or worse, into the open Gulf."

"Done that."

I ran to the canoe. Plato came out of the woods and ran with me. He hopped in as I pushed it to the water. The two life jackets were in the back, and I had my cell phone. I figured that's all I would need.

I paddled to the mouth of the river and looked as far into the bay as I could. No small boats appeared. Turning back, I headed slowly upstream, scouring the banks for boats and bodies. "Tell me if you notice anything," I said to Plato who stood sniffing the air at the front. He did what most dogs do out of car windows.

I passed some other canoers and kayakers, people who had rented them out for the day and moved around while the currents were gentle. I stopped a couple and asked if they'd seen a motor boat with a stocky, elderly man in it. None had.

I passed the camp going the other way until I reached the rental ramp. One man was working with a boat near the water.

"You rented a motor boat to a Mr. O'Neil?"

"Yeah," he said. "I hear they're looking for him. What's he done?"

"Nothing. His wife died, and they think he may be suicidal."

The man stopped and paled. "Oh, damn! I'd better tell the boss. He'll want to search." He wound a rope around a post and took off for the office. I left him, and turned around to scour the banks once again.

The grass at the bank waved with the beginnings of the tidal currents that would move in soon. I slowed for overhanging limbs and made sure it was moss that dragged against my head and not some arboreal reptile. Plato continued to stretch his neck and sniff the air. I had no idea what he might do if a snake did drop into the boat.

I found myself back in the wide part of the river where I had seen Vernon and others place the body of Cardel onto the police boat. The narrow lane that led to the small island was just before that. I turned around again and headed that way. If O'Neil's motor boat had been a small one, he could have moved this way. The currents were moving fast now, and I had to row hard to keep from being pushed into one of the muddy banks. Plato raised his nose higher and sniffed into the limbs that I had to duck.

When I came to the end of the lane, the currents moved me slightly to the right without my help. I was in the bayou that surrounded the tiny isle. It looked no different. A nesting egret poked in the grass for things to eat. One took off in flight. I moved with the currents around the isle where a black anhinga bird stretched its wings to dry. On the other side would be another lane that would push me into the Palmetto River. I wanted to make a full circle of the isle before I went there.

Plato gave a bark and looked toward the bank at the point of the isle we were approaching. A motor boat rested there, about to be carried out by the currents. It hadn't been tied or anchored in any way. Moving past it, I spied him.

O'Neil's stocky body sat among the reeds and grasses a few feet from the water. His knees and belly were muddy, like he had crawled ashore. He stared into the water, but I could see from his chest movement that he was breathing.

I pulled the canoe directly before him, letting the front rest on the bank. To keep it still, I had to continue maneuvering the paddle. The tide would soon raise me past the mud line.

"Are you okay, O'Neil?"

The man moved his glazed eyes toward me and for a moment,

I thought he had lost contact with reality. He finally gave a signal by shaking his head.

"She's dead, isn't she?"

I couldn't say it, but nodded.

"Just when her readings were going so well, she had to die." He looked at his hands and swiped them across his shirt. "I helped her, you know."

"How?"

"You don't think I really believed in all that voodoo stuff that predicted the future, do you? That Cardel woman was uptight most of the time. She was looking for doom, and we knew it. Sheila kept telling her something ill would happen with water. The woman believed it and kept going back." He laughed then, a cynical sound in spite of the presence of an angelic white egret behind him.

I touched Plato's back and whispered for him to sit. I didn't want him running about the nests right now. He glanced back at me and obeyed.

"But how long would she keep coming back?" O'Neil asked. "When would she get it that the whole thing was fake and she was wasting her money?" He looked at his hands again. "I have strong arms and hands, you know. My male upper body strength didn't fade with age."

A chill passed over me.

"I made sure the bad omen came true, you see."

I held the oar tighter. "Did you do something to Ben Cardel?" I was taking a chance, but I figured his upper body strength couldn't reach me before I shoved back into the fast moving current.

"I heard the woman say he was due in one night. I met him at the dock in a rented boat pretty much like that one." He pointed to the motor boat that now bounced in the currents and threatened to head into the water lane at any moment. "He wanted to get a drink before going home. Needed fortitude to face his wife, he said. I showed him a bottle I had in the boat. We came here. Right here on this little bird nest island and drank. Or, he drank. I pretended to. I had a broken oak limb in the boat. He never saw it. I had some oars, too, but I never had to use them."

O'Neil moved to a squatting position. "I just took the limb and slammed it against his sotted head. A couple more, and he was done."

He smiled and sat back in the mud. "My wife had proof she was a fortune teller, a seer. Belinda Cardell had her belief fulfilled." O'Neil's eyes met mine. "Plus, she escaped a sailor's beating that night. I figure I did her a favor."

We sat in silence, staring at each other. Plato didn't move at first. When he began looking back at me and whining, I flinched.

"Jimpson at the bait and tackle shop died the same way, didn't he?"

O'Neil's eyes widened. He stood and turned a circle in the mud. When he finally sat down again, he seemed resigned to talk.

"The man saw us come here," he said, facing the ground. "I stopped by there on my way back to the camp. He joked about me taking up drinking with an already drunken sailor. Wanted to know where I dropped him off or was I going to make the man swim home." O'Neil stared into the air. "Don't ask me why, but I kept that oak limb. I got it from the boat and went back. Jimpson didn't know I was coming. He'd gone to the back to do something and I just took advantage when he was leaning over." After a moment, he made one last comment. "Old man like that doesn't take much to kill."

O'Neil seemed almost comatose for a moment. I lifted the

cell phone and spoke as quietly as possible on a bayou running with tidal currents. "Vernon. We're on the little isle in the bayou. He's here. You'll need handcuffs."

The sheriff's boats were in the area already and sirens wailed enough for Plato to howl with them. O'Neil didn't seem to hear them. He sat perfectly still, even when a dragon fly lit on his folded hands.

There was no commotion or roughness when the deputies took O'Neil. They cuffed him in case he tried to swing at them. Even they recognized the upper body strength in the man.

One deputy tied the motor boat to a police boat and towed it in as evidence. My own canoe drifted back into the lane as the tide reached its highest on the bank. Plato was itching to jump off and help the two crime scene techs search the grass. Vernon winked at me when he saw Tony glare my way. It had happened before, and Tony's little nerve that said "adjuncts weren't supposed to find killers" jumped in his neck.

"I guess Pasquin and his friends will have the river funeral now," I said as I left the isle. Plato barked in agreement.

CHAPTER TWENTY

Sheila O'Neil's body was cremated and shipped back to some distant relatives in New York. Her husband said he wanted nothing to do with the remains. If he couldn't have Sheila live and in the flesh, she wasn't Sheila.

Marci Doucet wore a black arm band and hung dried funeral flowers over the reading door for a few days. Then she advertised for readers. Her shop filled with ladies of all ages. She even had two men apply, one a cross dresser whose witchy outfit could compete in any fashion contest. I joined Harold outside his store—along with Pasquin—to watch the parade going in for interviews.

Pasquin said the plans for Jimpson's funeral were made. It was now just a matter of time until the body would be released.

"You need to be part of it," he said to me one night outside the trailer. "You found his killer. You're kind of a spirit now."

"You sound like a fortune teller, old man. Maybe you should apply at Miss Doucet's place."

Harold said there was only one prediction that anyone could make with certainty. "Death," he said. "We're all going to die and it doesn't matter how. Cardel's widow might have benefited from her husband's killing, but it will only be temporary. She'll die someday soon. Can't take that money with you, no sir."

"What money?" I asked.

"She had insurance on the fellow. All the fish wives do. She'll do all right. Probably even better now that no one is drinking up the profits."

"Will she stay in that little house?" asked Pasquin.

"So far." Harold pointed a finger at a heavy woman in long black silky stuff. She wore a huge gardenia in her cleavage and had her nails painted a deep blood red. "Would you want something like that telling your future?"

"Well," said Pasquin, "it looks like she could tell you that you were going to die."

The two men laughed. The heavy woman shot them an evil eye with her hand as she entered Marci's shop.

I wandered off, leaving the two men to analyze every interviewee that came down the walk. A glass of tea at Kayleen's felt right about now, and I drifted in that direction. The bustle of the opening day had worn off, but she seemed to have a steady clientele at meal times.

"Will you be able to keep up the cooking pace?" I asked as I sat at one of her tables. "It seems a lot of work."

"It is, but it's my work," she said. "All those years of waiting tables at other people's places, now that was work. At least here, the tiredness belongs to me."

She sat across from me with a steaming cup of espresso. "I've come to love this strong brew," she said. "Most of the people who order it are not Americans. They tend to be Portuguese or from some other country, men who work the boats."

Her eyes lifted up and back a few times.

"You didn't sit here to tell me about sailors' drinking habits, did you?"

"Not really. I needed to explain about—that night."

"You don't have to. I can understand your need for the handsome Mr. Doucet."

She smiled. "And it is a need. Bub spends most of his time at the boat repair. He's not much interested in me anymore."

"Nor you him," I said.

She nodded. "A hunk like Bernard comes along...well, it happens."

"A hunk, yes. Did he ever mention that he did amateur boxing?"

Her eyes opened wide. "Why no. He never said. Of course, he hasn't said much about his life before coming here. He was on a boat when Katrina hit, but they were able to find refuge off Texas. I think he lived on that boat until his sister got a place here."

"And that was his only job?"

"As far as I know." She leaned over and touched my hand. "Look, Luanne, when you need someone for this particular need, you don't much care about their employment history."

I smiled. "I guess not. Maybe I heard wrong. It must have been some other seaman who boxed."

"I'd say so. He sure doesn't have any marks on him from a beating of that nature." She laughed and I joined her.

Three women came into the café. Each was dressed in black and they appeared to be related. I figured Grandma, Mother, and daughter had applied to do familial readings at the Talisman. That would be a gimmick, at least.

"Excuse me," said Kayleen as she rose to wait on them. "They'll want tea. Herbals. I've had to stock a few since Marci's place has become so popular."

Yes, I thought, *and I bet you bought them from her rather than a wholesale house.*

All the talk about Bernard reminded me of the bookends again. I made a quick call to Marshall.

"Nice boyfriend you got there. He got the order to run the tests. Too bad it didn't turn out the way you wanted."

"Meaning you got no prints?"

"Crude partials that are almost impossible to match. You need to find some fat tomes to put between these and forget about evidence."

I finished my iced tea and strolled back toward Harold's. Marci's line of would-be seers had vanished, and I wondered who we'd see next in Sheila's sad little room.

"Not all finished yet," said Pasquin as I approached the two men, still in their chairs.

I followed his pointing finger to see a tall mulatto woman with a head scarf and flashing earrings. She wore orange Capri pants and a matching tee shirt. Behind her were two men who didn't look like sailors. As she came closer to the Doucet shop, I felt she looked familiar. I touched my holy shrimp, feeling its outline beneath my shirt.

"I'll be back," I said.

I entered the shop ahead of the woman. Marci was talking with another woman, one who was a bit on the elderly side. She was thin and had unkempt gray hair. A little costuming would turn her into a hag from the forest for sure.

I placed myself behind a stack of books near the door and watched the woman enter. Her two companions stood outside, one on each side.

"You stole my money!" The woman said in a loud voice. She pointed a long finger at Marci.

Marci paled and darted for the back of her counter. The elderly woman said "wait" in a small voice.

"You went back to the shop after the storm and took it all out of the safe!" The shout was louder this time.

Marci didn't play her coy game this time. I saw her reach for something beneath the counter.

"Don't try and use your battering rams on me. I've got my own." She pointed to the men outside the door.

Marci froze and stared at the men. They stood like palace guards with their hands behind their backs.

The woman began to move through the shop. "Just look at this stuff. All mine. And the talisman box!" She pointed to the one where Pasquin had found my holy shrimp. "You took that right off the wall." I noticed her pointing finger had a long nail painted black with a gold dot at the tip. Her other nails were painted red.

"I—I had no idea you were alive, Janine," said Marci. One hand still resting beneath the counter. "The shop was destroyed."

"You knew I was alive. I had my relatives tell you to salvage as much as possible and wait for me."

"I never got such a message." Marci blinked back tears.

"Oh yes you did!" Janine screamed. She moved again through the shop, stopping once to glare at the old woman. Glancing up at the sign over the reader's door, she looked back and laughed. "Is this what you've got to do Tarot readings?" She didn't explain but found a basket of amulets and gasped. "That's even mine!" She made a big sweeping motion and knocked the whole business to the floor. Some hit the elderly lady's legs before landing with a bang.

The men outside turned when they heard the noise but they made no moves. I figured they were waiting for a signal. It was time for me to act. I pulled out my phone and ran an SOS text to Vernon. We had always talked about doing that in case we couldn't talk in private. He wouldn't answer, just come. At least I was hoping he read it right away. He wasn't always in a position to do so.

"You were nothing but a wimpy little girl," said Janine. "I helped you get a start and look what you did." She continued to sweep things to the floor. So far, they were displays and baskets of things. When she started turning over book racks and breaking glass, I planned to duck out the back and pull the old lady with me.

"Open that register!" Janine yelled at Marci. The two women stood facing each other now. Janine had considerable height on Marci, not to mention a stronger body. If this turned into a female cat fight, Marci was going to get the scars.

"I won't! I earned every bit of that cash, and you're not getting it."

"You see those fellows outside? They know what you did. They're going to come in here and help ruin this place. You stole from me and I plan to take it all back!"

"There are witnesses," she said.

"What! That old lady?" Janine approached the woman again and leaned over her. "Boo!" she said close to her face. The woman flinched and fell backwards.

Marci darted her eyes toward me, but Janine didn't follow. I sighed with relief that she didn't know I was there. I squatted behind the books. If the men outside turned and looked into the window, they might see me. I hit the SOS text again, this time to Tony. I had to take the chance that he might call, but right now, a war was going to break out any minute.

Janine laughed at the woman on the floor and began really slamming things about. As long as no one interfered, it looked as though she would do it all herself. I heard a siren in the distance and prayed it was for here and not some boating accident.

It came closer, and the men turned toward the shop. One

reached for the door, but I leapt and turned the bolt before he could make it. He shook the handle. The other one tried breaking it with his foot but the glass was too strong. Before trying again, the sheriff's car came into view, and he tripped as he turned to run. The other one darted toward Harold's. I drew in my breath and hoped the two old men had sense enough to stay out of their way.

I jerked the old lady off the floor and pulled her out the back door. Inside, I could hear the physical fight begin. Both women screamed. Janine let out a string of curses, and they weren't spells. Marci limited her cries to "No!" and "Help!"

I went back in and ran to the front door to unlock it. Vernon was there with another deputy, guns drawn. When they realized that wasn't the force needed, they used their hands to grab both of Janine's and handcuff her. Marci took advantage and tore at the woman. Vernon pushed her back behind the counter.

"You'd best handcuff her, too," I said. "There's an accusation of theft here."

Vernon called for backup and it arrived before he put his phone away. Tony rushed in to find two women throwing verbal insults at each other and a destroyed shop.

"We got this one up the walk," said a deputy who brought in one of the guards. "Some old man stuck out a piece of iron and tripped him."

Vernon's mouth jumped at the corners. He'd laugh about it later, but he knew the old swamp rats had struck again.

"There's another one," I said.

"We're after him." The deputy took a look at the damage and pulled his prisoner to a car.

When the women and both men had been read their rights, they were arrested for public disturbance and taken away.

"It will become much more than that," I said to Vernon who stayed behind and made a report on the damage. He took a statement from the old lady and called a relative to come and get her. She decided to hell with fortune telling.

"It looks like Zeke Owen was hired to find Marci Doucet, not Janine Guerrin. I'll bet the story of how Marci got away with the shop fortune after Katrina will be quite a tale."

"And managed to hide it all these years," said Vernon. "Oh, yeah, I've got some information Tony found on Bernard."

Bernard hadn't made an appearance. If he wasn't on his boat, could he have known of this confrontation?

I left the deputies to tape off the shop and wandered back to Harold's Oddities. Pasquin and Harold were still in their chairs.

"So which one of you tripped the runner?" I asked.

"I tippy toed to the back door when I heard the shouting," said Pasquin. "Came back here and told Harold nothing good was happening down there. He called 911."

"And got me a rod from inside. Don't tell me this stuff is junk." He laughed. "I was planning on cracking some heads, but this fellow came running this way. Just tossed it between his legs and down he went. Glad I didn't have to sit on him. The deputy was close."

I sighed with relief. Besides my texts, Harold had called in help. I smiled and shook his hand.

"Don't I get a shake, too?" said Pasquin.

I took his hat and slapped his knee. I didn't say anything, just walked away with a lump in my throat.

CHAPTER TWENTY-ONE

Vernon and I sat in the tiny trailer with carry out plates of fish from Kayleen's. It nearly equaled Mama's in quality since the fish was delivered daily from Crusty Dock.

"Okay, you want to hear about the Doucet data?"

I nodded and watched as Vernon took a folder from a case he carried inside, not something he often did.

"He did do amateur bantam weight boxing a while back. He began working on a Tom Kingston…"

"This Tom Kingston, who is he?"

"No one now. He owned a lot of boats maybe twenty years ago. Some were shrimp boats. He had his initials put in brass on all of them. When his widow sold them off, they became known as Tom Kingston boats."

"Sold off to whom?"

"Anyone who would buy them. They're sturdy craft. Bernard Doucet had been hurt on a previous job when some rigging fell on his shoulder and leg. Wrecked the strength in one arm and gave him a permanent limp. He's been getting monthly disability payments for a long time. Looks like he used it to put a down payment on his own boat."

"The Talisman?"

"Yes, eventually. He first bought a different, cheaper boat. He sold that one and bought The Talisman. He made a deal with the buyer of the first boat for payments to come in monthly rather than a big payment up front. He's still getting them."

I nodded. Bernard, the beautiful, has his own money-making boat, payments for an older one coming every month, and disability along with it all.

"If he's got a disability in his shoulder and leg, he's good at covering them," I said, remembering him carrying off the iron table frames, one in each hand.

"I guess he can afford Marci's lawyer."

"Marci is quite a different story." Vernon picked up the folder and pulled out a photograph. "There's your boxer."

I stared at the black and white. A referee stood in the middle of a boxing arena. His arms were around two men in boxing gloves. Their trainers stood on each side of them.

"This fight was a draw."

"This fight was not fought by the Bernard Doucet I know."

The two boxers were shorter than the referee. Their stocky builds reminded me of what O'Neil might have looked like at that age. The one that was supposed to be Bernard Doucet had light hair, a wispy sort of stuff that stood around his head like a halo. His features were thin.

"Did he suddenly become tall and ethnic in the last few years?"

Vernon smiled at me. "You've guessed we've got an imposter."

"If this is the real one, yes, we do."

"Tony chewed his jaw when I showed him this and reminded him that you asked for the information."

"And is he still chewing it?"

"You notice he let me bring you the picture instead of bringing it himself. He would have if this had been some Latin-looking boxer."

"I'd say this guy is the real brother." I tapped the picture. "He looks more like Marci. All light and ethereal."

"Like a pretty little butterfly." Vernon smiled without looking at me.

"Pretty little butterflies have a grotesque caterpillar down their middles," I said. "Now who is the other Bernard?"

"A boyfriend, perhaps?"

"Boyfriend? He's been doing the nasty with Kayleen. Marci would put up with that?"

"She had something to hide besides a false brother," said Vernon. He frowned. "Seriously, we need to find this brother. There is no record of him after he starts shrimping with The Talisman. If he's still out there, he's keeping it legal, or at least quiet."

"Legal? With a stealing sister like Marci?"

"We've got the Coast Guard alerted and a lookout at Crusty Dock."

"There are more places than Crusty to bring shrimp loads to shore," I said.

"Lots more, and we've got word out to watch for that boat, but we don't have enough people to watch all the docks. Besides, he could be keeping himself on the Texas side of the Gulf."

"Some men were in the shop looking for Bernard. They said they were holding up the ship for him."

"Not The Talisman. Not unless it was out in the bay and they planned to meet it in a smaller boat."

"Where is the tall and dark Bernard right now?" I asked

"We can't seem to find him. Maybe he got on that boat."

"Or maybe Miss Kayleen is hiding him in her pantry."

Vernon smiled. "We do have enough men to watch that place."

"Okay. So he's on a boat somewhere, probably under his own name. If her brother is out there, too, why does he need to use that name while he's ashore?"

We left the question open. There were too many maybes. If Kayleen knew the truth, she wasn't going to give up her newly found thrill in the sack. Marci surely wouldn't tell on whoever it was that was living in her trailer.

Plato joined us for the night. The closeness was nice, maybe too nice. The narrow beds, the noisy air conditioner, the dog that had to be stepped over to get to the bathroom. Not for the first time, I longed for my comfortable and roomy swamp house.

"Do you think the green lizards have set up colonies in my living room?" I whispered to Vernon.

"In your kitchen, most likely," he whispered back.

"Vernon," I said.

"Go to sleep."

"Are you tying the arm bones and skull to O'Neil?"

"I'm not tying them to anything." He mumbled, his mouth buried in the sheets.

"The arm and hand bones were wrapped in a coat too large for the person who owned them, right?"

"Why?"

"And there was no evidence that the skull had been bashed like Cardel and Jimpson."

"Are you going to answer me or keep me awake all night."

I looked at him. "The coat. It might fit the second Bernard Doucet, right?"

Vernon sat up straight. "Why should I get any sleep? Why should Tony?" He pulled his phone from the little side table and hit a number.

"I'm going to tell him you made me do this."

I smiled. "Why not? He thinks I'm just the maid that takes care of this little police trailer, does the mopping and the dusting, and…" I stopped when Vernon let me know Tony had picked up the phone.

"Was he really sound asleep?" I smiled as I handed over a cup of steaming coffee to Vernon the next morning.

"Said he was."

Vernon wasn't going to begin his day by Tony bashing no matter how much I wanted to hear what he said about it. He had told Tony that "Luanne is the one who came up with this."

"Tony will question Marci this morning. He wants you to come in and make a statement about what you saw happen between the two women." He smiled at his cup. "I suggest you get on to the sheriff's office and do that. You might be in time to hear her questioned."

"Do they have a case? I mean it was the other woman who barged in and started fighting."

He nodded and gulped the last of his coffee. "But she's accusing Marci of stealing. Tony is getting touch with New Orleans Police today."

"The phony brother issue has to be dealt with one day."

"That, too." He kissed my cheek and headed for the patrol car.

I drove to the Sheriff's office where Tony paced the floor of his office. He spoke on the phone to New Orleans, complaining that no one seemed to have anything on the Guerrin family nor the business Janine owned.

"Don't you keep records in your state capital?" He said. "That didn't wash away in the storm."

He rolled his eyes as someone on the other end tried to answer him.

"I can't believe they can't find anything in this day of high tech. A business license should be on file somewhere in that state." He sat down hard in his rolling chair.

"Maybe she never got a license." I eyed a chair full of folders and decided to lean against the wall. "A little shop like that, maybe Janine just took it over."

Tony glared at me without saying a word. "She's filing papers against the Doucet woman, saying she took money from the safe after the storm and ran away with it."

"Won't the New Orleans Police have to deal with that?"

"You can bet we won't. Except, of course, as her motive for trashing the shop."

"Isn't there more to this mess? What about the Doucet brother. Surely, you don't believe that dark, handsome fellow is who he says he is."

Tony nodded without looking at me. "We'll ask her about that, too, but she's lawyered up already. I'd rather keep the two subjects separate right now."

He picked up the phone and called for a recorder. I responded by giving him a formal statement of what I saw happen in The Talisman shop.

"How come you didn't bring those two old men in with you?" said Tony. "We need formal statements from them about anything they saw, including tripping up one of the guards when he ran."

"I would have brought them had you told me to," I said.

He looked at me as though I should have known better. Deep down, it was a criticism of himself. Not that he criticized himself for forgetting to tell me, but that I had to remind him of such forgetfulness. Tony wasn't all that complicated.

I leaned forward and in my best humble voice asked, "Is there any way to compare the DNA of the arm and skull bones to Marci Doucet's?"

Tony looked at me in surprise, then scowled for a second. "You think they are related?"

I shrugged. "All I know is that the current carrier of name, Bernard Doucet, is probably not her brother. He says he was on The Talisman, where the brother is supposed to be. Arm bones in an oversized coat turn up in the water, possibly washed in from the bay on the tide. The bones are probably male, and they are from a small sized male. I'd say they match Bernard Doucet's body structure, the real Bernard Doucet."

Tony grabbed the telephone and poked at a number frequently called. He then put it on conference call and sat back in his chair.

"I've got Luanne in the office," he said to Marshall Long.

"Lucky you!"

"Cut the stuff, Long. What do you have on the DNA from the arm bones and skull?"

"You got a minute? I'm digging it out of the envelope right now?"

"Only a minute."

I smiled to myself. This male act of pushing each other to the edge was their Alpha male battle, seeing who could run this case the best.

"Just what I thought. Skull and arms and hands all belong to each other." Another shuffle of papers came across the line. "No match nationally that they can find. We don't know who he is, but we've got only one person." Marshall moved papers around again. "You know. Get Luanne back out there and find the rest of the guy."

"We," Tony looked up at me and corrected himself, "she has someone she wants you to match that DNA against."

"Yeah? You got somebody to swab the cheek or draw the blood?"

"It won't be that easy. This may be something we'll have to snatch—like a drinking glass."

"Just be sure it's not contaminated with someone else's spit." Marshall laughed at his own joke.

Tony turned off the phone and leaned back in his chair. "Just what do you know about this other Bernard, the visible one?"

"Not much. Seems a lady's man. Two fishermen types were looking for him to rejoin the boat, The Talisman, and get back to work. I do know he's been giving Kayleen some jollies lately. As much as I hate to expose her little affair, I'd talk to her if I had a badge."

"Your," he stopped himself, "Vernon has a badge."

"Yes, and he'll question her if you say so. Might, however, be less familiar and perhaps more intimidating if you did it." I smiled at him. I knew he'd love being "intimidating."

"She'll be at the café, right?"

I left Tony's office, knowing he'd show up at Kayleen's in a matter of moments. Marci Doucet's brother—false or real— wasn't really an aspect of the case with Janine, at least not yet. It was looking more like an aspect of the bones in the water case. In my head, I was betting the two would come together some-how.

Before I headed back to the tiny trailer that was becoming an abysmal jail-cell, I stopped at Mama's Table.

"What do you think of Kayleen's prospects of keeping things going at Ciel?"

"She's got a good sturdy place and she's a good cook. Needs a bit more organized help, but that will come with practice." Mama shoved a plate of fried catfish in front of me. "Fresh," she said. "Now. Her problem is going to be with that husband of hers. He's got a fuse that seems lit about all the time. Not much patience with a woman doing better than he is."

"Even with money coming in?"

"If it was only coming in, he'd be right with it. But in this business, it's got to go out, too. Upkeep, overhead, new supplies. Keeping up with licenses and the health department. You can work around all that, but Bub has no sense of business. He's used to working for somebody else. He gets his hands greasy at that boat repair place but he never has to put out money to buy new grease, or rivets, or whatever they use. He whines and grumbles every time Kayleen needs something."

I nodded. "What kind of relationship do they have—otherwise?" I winked at her.

"You're bring up stuff I'm not part of, Luanne."

"I'm asking for a reason."

"I heard about her little escapade with Bernard Doucet. He was around all day on her opening. In fact, I don't know how we'd have got it all done without him."

"And Marci didn't care?"

Mama shrugged. "She never came near the café. I guessed she didn't mind letting her brother help a place that was certain to bring in customers to her own place."

"Her brother?"

Mama gave me a look without asking the question. "They don't look much alike, do they?"

CHAPTER TWENTY-TWO

Just as I suspected, Tony's unmarked car sat in the parking area outside Kayleen's Café. He had arrived while I ate catfish with Mama. I parked the Honda next to his car and walked inside, hoping to get something out of him when he finished talking to her.

"How the hell would I know about his family?" I heard Kayleen yelling from the kitchen area. "You want to talk to me, why don't you do it somewhere private?"

I eased past the counter and stood in the doorway that led into the work area of the kitchen. One of the hired workers swept the floor while two others washed shrimp at an industrial sink.

Tony stood in the kitchen in his crisp pants and shirt, his hair combed to perfection, and sweat running down his forehead. It amazed me that he tried questioning Kayleen alone.

"Maybe you could sit at one of the tables," I said when silence had gone on too long. "There are no customers right now."

Kayleen jerked off her apron and tossed it on a table. She stomped out of the kitchen. "And there won't be very many if the law keeps showing up here." She stopped and turned to face Tony who nearly ran into her. "If I lose money because of you guys, so help me…" She didn't finish but turned and found a table near the storage room.

Tony looked at me and nodded for me to follow him.

When we were all seated around the table, I looked at the storage room door. It was closed, but Kayleen saw me.

"All right! You caught us there. We had an attraction to each other and indulged in a little adultery." She stared at Tony. "Now unless you're some church freak who plans on crucifying me for that, you'd better have something pretty good to say."

Tony took a deep breath and tried to glare at her. "I don't care how much adultery you commit. I'm here to find out what you know about this guy. We've got reasons for wanting to know, and I cannot tell you what they are right now."

"Please, Kayleen," I said. "It's important to another case. It doesn't involve you, but given that you're kind of friendly with the guy, the sheriff thinks he may have told you other things."

She sat up straight. "Like what?"

"Has he ever said anything about his parents or his childhood with Marci, things like that?"

She smiled and nodded. "Oh, I see. You think this has something to do with that woman who beat up Marci and nearly destroyed her shop." She frowned then and sat quiet for a moment. "It may have, in fact. You know what? I haven't seen the guy since that happened. Not a word even."

"You have a phone number for him?"

She shook her head. "We didn't risk that. He said he didn't carry one anyway."

"Was Marci ever here in the restaurant with him?"

She shook her head again. "That woman never has been here except once when she was looking for him." She grinned. "Fortunately, he wasn't here at the time."

Tony cleared his throat. "I need to ask you this, Kayleen." Without looking at her, he said, "Do you think he has other, well, lovers?"

Kayleen glared at him, then seemed to wilt. "Look. He's gorgeous, has all the flattering little moves a woman wants, and he's fairly generous with his time. Not to mention being really good in…" She stopped and looked at Tony and me. "You know. Do I think he's had others? Plenty. He's not the kind who has to do without."

"And your husband?" asked Tony. "What does he know about this?"

I knew then where Tony was headed. He wanted to know if Bub could have done away with the guy. It would have been typical of some Southern male to take that route, especially one who was insecure and no stud himself.

"Bub? He wouldn't know unless I paid the guy, and then it would be the money not the guy that would get to him."

"Where is your husband now?"

"He's begun sitting on his bottom at the place where he works, the boat repair yard at Crusty Dock. I guess he got tired of sitting on it at the trailer camp. Gibson has sworn off liquor for now. Bub says he's not fun anymore."

"So he can't work with his broken arm, but prefers to watch others fix the boats?" I said.

"Yeah. The smell of oil is sweeter to him than the smell of perfume."

Mama was right. If Kayleen's place failed, it was going to be a problem with Bub that did it.

"Do you have any idea where we could find Marci's brother right now?"

"No," Kayleen said and looked down at the table top. "Guess the attraction here wasn't enough for him." She turned her head toward the kitchen, revealing watery eyes. "I need to get in there.

We'll have a big lunch crowd soon."

Tony made it clear to her that she needed to call if she saw Bernard, and to keep it from him. We headed to the parking lot.

A call came to Tony's phone while we were standing there. He ended it with "so it's a standoff for now."

"Seems the Guerrin woman has filed charges against the Doucet woman for stealing and the Doucet woman has filed charges against the Guerrin woman for destroying her shop. Lawyers are in on it. It'll take a judge to sort it all out now."

"What about O'Neil? Will he go to trial soon?"

"Not sure. I'm heading back to the trailer camp to wait for the evidence people to collect his trailer. We'll take it back and search it thoroughly there."

"I thought you'd done that."

"Preliminary search, yes. We won't find anything. I believe the guy's confession. But we can't leave it and get accused later of sloppy police work."

"Won't you have to do the same with Marci's trailer?"

"Hah! That will really be a warrant here, a warrant there, situation. The Geurrin people will want to know if she's got anything from the New Orleans shop inside that place. Of course, the shop will be searched, too."

I followed him back to the camp, and sat next to him in the O'Neils' chairs, waiting for the truck to take the trailer as evidence.

We were fanning ourselves and suggesting that we retreat to the tiny trailer for air conditioning when a shiny new white van pulled into the area. Belinda Cardel eased out the driver's side. She saw us and smiled. Her hair had been trimmed to a boyish cut that made the lined face look a few years younger.

She passed us and stood in front of the O'Neil trailer. "I just wanted to see where the woman lived," she said. "I've seen it before, but not up close."

Tony and I watched her stare at the vehicle and move her eyes from end to end.

"I wonder if she knew what her husband was going to do or if she knew what would happen, to both husbands."

"To yours and hers?" I asked. "Did she ever hint that she knew what her husband was planning to do?"

"Not what he actually did, but she did say a couple of times that he just couldn't live without her, that he'd just die if anything happened to her."

"And did she indicate something was going to happen to her." I kept talking, and Tony just glanced at me.

"No. I never knew she was sick. I guess I should have read into that remark, but I was too concerned for my own predictions."

"Nice car you've got there," said Tony.

Belinda smiled and I noticed she actually wore lipstick. "I bought it with insurance money. Ben would have wanted me to get a better car."

"I'll bet he would," I said under my breath but loud enough for Tony to hear. "From what I heard, he would have made her walk everywhere."

"It's the way she wants to remember him," said Tony.

A flat bed truck pulled into the area and blew its horn for someone to remove the white van.

"You'll have to pull it out of the way," said Tony. "We're taking away the trailer. It's evidence now."

"Oh, you are the deputy, aren't you?" Belinda acted surprised.

"Detective, ma'am," he said. "The van?"

She hurried to her van and pulled it under a tree.

The men with the flatbed backed up to the O'Neil trailer, and with gloved hands, attached it to the pulleys that would load it for transport. A third man who had followed in a small car, got out and closely searched the concrete slab and the space around it. He pronounced the hookups no longer hooked up and gave the okay to go with the trailer. In a matter of moments, the only things left of the O'Neils were their two chairs. Tony said they wouldn't be useful, but he'd toss them in his trunk and take them to the lab.

The air was dryer today, and there didn't seem to be any rain in the distant white clouds. I couldn't bear the thought of sitting inside that trailer and instead took a walk along the river bank. I didn't get far. A familiar putt-putt pulled close to the landing.

"You want to join us?" said Pasquin. He held the boat steady, while Harold held on to his seat with both hands.

"You better come along because I don't swim," said the man with a big grin. "Old Cajun here won't be able to save me if I fall in."

"You don't swim? And you were in the military?"

"Military back then," he said. "I don't think they cared. Besides, I kind of faked it."

I walked to the canoe and grabbed a life jacket. Tossing it to him, I eased into the boat with the two old men.

"He won't wear one," I said, pointing to Pasquin. "I don't even know if he could, or would, swim."

"Been swimming since I was a boy," he said and laughed.

It had been my fear ever since I'd known him that he'd fall into the water and drown or be chomped on by a gator. I'd given up worrying, because he wasn't going to put on the jacket. Too hot, he said.

"Where are you two going?"

"Nowhere in particular," said Pasquin. "I been promising this old guy a ride in my boat, and things are slow up at his boutique today." They both laughed.

"Not sure I can stand the comedy, but let's go." I helped Harold with the jacket.

"I want to see where they found Cardel's body and the killer," said Harold. "Kind of like those crime documentaries on television, only this is real."

Pasquin turned the boat toward the lane that would run between the river and the small isle. Along the shore, we saw lone fishermen, old men, with poles in the water. One man had a string of fish. He and Pasquin saluted each other.

"I suppose you know most of these people?" I said.

"Most, yep." He didn't go any further. Just fellow swampers who lazed around on days like this.

We came to the water lane and Pasquin made the turn.

"What are you going to do about getting around them limbs?" asked Harold.

"Duck. Move them out of the way," said Pasquin. "Just get beneath them one way or the other."

Harold looked nervous, but I helped him by holding the limb and letting him bend to his knees until we passed the tree growth.

"This is better," he said when we hit the bayou. "And that's the little island where it all happened, right?" He pointed to the clump of dirt with a heavy growth of grasses and muddy banks. An egrett flew up when it felt the vibration of the motor, its wide white wings looking like an angel on its way to heaven.

That happened several times as Pasquin made his way around the island. Every time, Harold made a sound like it was something good to eat. "Mmm, yes," he'd say in a whisper. "Pretty stuff."

"Here it is," I said. "The place where Vernon said the body was lying." I pointed to an area where the grass had been mashed down some. It was already growing back to the heights before trauma had hit it. "And O'Neil was not far away when I found him sitting on the island. He'd given up completely, even given up killing himself."

"He won't last long in prison," said Harold. "Nasty place, and an old man like that." He sat still and quiet for a moment, a downturned expression. "Balogna sandwiches will kill him."

Pasquin laughed first. Harold followed. I just shrugged.

Pasquin made one more complete circle of the island. "You keep going that way and you'll come to our river, the Palmetto," he said. "That's where we plan to start the funeral procession."

"Not on the St. Margaret's?" I asked. "In front of his own place?"

"Nope. He was killed there. The Palmetto is where most of his friends fished. We'll send him off on the place where we know he enjoyed life."

"And drop his ashes there, too?"

"At the very end, where the bay meets the river. He liked watching the manatees down there." Pasquin suddenly pulled his hat down a bit further. I knew he was shading his eyes that had watered up. He regained his composure, but his voice was a bit more husky. "We'll put him down there with them."

Pasquin wasn't ready to go back to the shops and headed up the St. Margaret's instead. He pointed out landings and small shacks along with some tall fancy houses on stilts, and knew all the owners' names. He even mentioned if they were big names in town, maybe a congressman or a car dealership owner. They were all equal to him, just more people who loved his neck of the swamp.

"Delivery dock coming up," he said in the manner of a tour

guide. He pointed to an ugly concrete block building built close to the water. It had a concrete platform next to a ramp. Small boats could be launched off the ramp, but the deep water in front of the platform would allow the bigger shrimp boats to unload their catch. No one seemed about the place.

"You watch," said Pasquin. "Somebody will put in pretty soon." He pulled his boat under a tree across the river so that we would be in full view of anything happening there.

"How soon?" said Harold after we had been sitting for nearly fifteen minutes. "It's buggy out here, and I'm not all that sure I want to see another boat right now."

Pasquin chuckled and started the engine. We moved slowly back down the river, staying in the center where he didn't have to dodge but a few cypress trees. Another motor boat came toward us. Two men sat, one steering, the other staring. As we passed, the one in the back stood part way up and looked directly at me.

"Hey!" I shouted. "Wait a minute."

Pasquin slowed, and Harold grabbed hold of his seat.

"You work with Mr. Doucet on The Talisman, right?" I yelled at the boat as it moved a bit faster. "Hold on a minute."

The man who stared at me waved his hand at his companion and yelled, "Go! Go!"

Pasquin backed up, nearly coming alongside the other boat. The man at the tiller woke up then and recognized me. He tried to speed up but did something with his finger. It came up dripping blood.

"Move it!" cried the other one.

I'm not sure why, but I reached out and grabbed the side of their boat, causing the two boats to bump. It tossed the would-be pilot off balance and he fell to one side. The other man, more afraid of me than of the impending dunk in swift water, pushed himself over to the throttle. He made the boat go fast, but he didn't guide it. It turned and rammed into the bank.

"Follow them!" I said to Pasquin, and pulled out my cell phone. I hit Tony's number and handed it to Harold. "Tell him where we are."

I had a short glimpse of Harold's bewildered face as I slid over the side. The staring man was doing his best to crawl out of the boat and up a slippery bank to refuge in the swamp. I was after him, hoping he wasn't going to fight me.

I didn't have to worry. He slipped twice, hitting his chin and biting his lip so badly that he dripped blood. I grabbed his shirt collar and pulled him into the water. He didn't like that, but at least I had him on familiar territory. He tossed and struggled, but I pulled him to Pasquin's boat. Both men leaned over and dragged him aboard.

"You planning on getting the other one?" said Harold. He pointed to the other man who sat horrified in mud and water. The engine on his boat had konked out.

I looked back as I held onto the side of Pasquin's boat. "What about it, fellow? Are you coming with us or do you want to wait for the cops right there on the bank?"

He shook his head. "I'm staying here. I won't run. Just don't pull me into that river."

I looked into Pasquin's boat. Three men, two very old ones and a young sailor. "For fishermen, you two don't seem happy with this water."

"Not river water," said the one on shore. "Never did like it. I can deal with the ocean, but not this stuff."

Harold had gotten through to Tony's number. Help arrived in a swarm of deputies in swamp buggies and river boats.

I rode back in a police boat, my clothes muddy and damp. The two men sat in the back, handcuffed but not under arrest. "We've got some questions," the deputy said. "And you two have this idea to run."

"Not me," said the former operator of the boat, his finger now bandaged from a first aid kit in the police boat. "I ain't about to jump off in this stuff."

CHAPTER TWENTY-THREE

At my landing near Fogarty Spring, I stood looking at my old swamp house, its fading white boards like palace walls to me. A patrol car waited in the road next to the landing. It would transport the two men to the sheriff's office. Another patrol car would pick me up after I showered and changed into dry clothes.

The screen porch was a bit sandy from not being swept in a while, and the house smelled a bit musty from the air conditioning set at a higher than usual temperature, but the place engulfed me the minute I walked through the door. It seeme huge, a place for each piece of furniture and more if I wanted it. The sound of my feet on the polished wood floors rang sweeter than flip flops on trailer linoleum any day. I rushed upstairs to the shower, the hot water from my own tank raining down on my muddy head.

"You like this place, I suppose?" A familiar voice sounded from the living room as I hurried into clean jeans.

"I knew they'd send you," I said as I glanced down the stairs at a grinning face and bald head. "Vernon to the rescue."

"You thought you'd be Tarzan and grab two monkeys out of the water."

"And I did."

We arrived at the office in time for the interviews, as Tony called them. The men would be interviewed separately. One was already asking for an attorney even though he wasn't under arrest. "I've got a maritime lawyer," he said.

Tony nodded at the deputy. "Just be sure to tell him you've not been arrested for anything."

The other man, the one with the cut finger and fear of river water, wasn't so keen on a maritime lawyer or any other kind. He was ready to talk and even said to be sure they got it all down.

Getting it down meant recording it. I sat behind the window with Vernon. Tony was in the room with the man and with Sergeant Loman, whose sleepy eyes looked as though he was bored with life. Those eyes had fooled more than one crook into believing he wasn't even listening.

"Okay," said Tony. "We want to know where Bernard Doucet is." He stared at the man.

In spite of offering to talk, the man looked about him, his eyes twitching.

"He's around but won't tell us where. I think he's afraid of what happened to his sister."

"He's afraid of Janine Guerrin?"

"Who?" The man looked a bit terrified now. "I don't know who that is."

"The woman who allegedly attacked Marci Doucet. That is who we're talking about here, isn't it?"

The nodded his head quickly. "Did she tear up the shop, too?"

"So I hear."

"See. He doesn't want any trouble. He doesn't want anything to interfere with the boat and the shrimp business."

"Bernard?"

The man blinked at Tony, then nodded. "He said if he got mixed up in some squabble of his sister's, he might be sued for the boat."

"I see," said Tony. "Does that mean the boat is in his sister's name, too?"

"I think so."

"I don't," said Tony. "We checked Bernard's background. He owns that boat all by himself."

The man's face paled. "I didn't know."

Tony stared at the man.

"Well, I know that it does belong to the sister. Yes, I know that." He bobbed his head but couldn't look at Tony.

Tony leaned back and placed his hands behind his neck. "I'm listening."

"See," he looked up to make sure Tony was seeing. "when a man dies, his next of kin usually inherits. Unless he has a will that says otherwise. But, there wasn't a will that said otherwise. Miss Doucet owns The Talisman."

Tony put his hands on the table. "You mean to tell me that Bernard is dead?"

He nodded again.

"Bernard Doucet, a tall dark man, well built, looks a bit Latino?"

This time the man's eyes opened wider and he shook his head.

"No. The one who is short and has coloring like his sister. He died several months back."

Tony sat staring quietly at the man. He finally took a deep breath and said, "Okay. Let's have the entire story from the start. From the time Bernard died, or was killed, or whatever."

This was the priestly order the man needed. It was confession time.

"We've been working the shrimp boats for Bernard Doucet for a long time. Way before he bought this boat. Business was pretty good, and he needed to hire on another hand. It was his sister who recommended somebody. He had experience and was in the area where we were at the time, off Texas." The man shuffled in his chair and cleared his throat. "He was this good looking guy, one of his sister's lovers, so Bernard said. And he was okay. Worked hard. Never got into fights or drank much. He'd go way off from us when we had shore days. Bernard said he liked the ladies. Didn't seem to bother him that his sister liked the guy. We went on like this for a while."

"Wait," said Tony. "Give me a time frame here. Is this before or after Katrina?"

"Way after. His sister was working in some kind of office around Mobile at the time. Not too much later—after the incident—she moved here."

"The incident?"

"I'm getting to that. See, it was winter and pretty cold in the northern Gulf. Bernard caught a bug of some kind, maybe a flu. He was moving us down the coast of Florida. Said the warmer air would make him well. It didn't. We decided to cross the Gulf, but Bernard got sicker. It must have turned into pneumonia or something. He went to his bed to rest and never came back. When we checked on him, he was dead, really dead."

"Wait. He died of the flu, you're saying? No one killed him?"

"No! We all liked him. Besides, there were only three of us and we were all above deck when he went to his bed."

"Okay. He's dead. What then?"

"We kept him wrapped up in a tarp and on ice for a long time." The man stared around the room. "It's not legal, you see, to keep a dead body like that where you keep shrimp that's going to be delivered to eating places."

"Not a bad law at all," said Tony.

"But we didn't have any shrimp or any other seafood on board at the time. Technically, they weren't stored together."

"Did you contact the sister?"

He nodded and put his head down. "That's when the deception began. It was their idea. Not mine. I followed orders."

"Whose? Your captain was dead."

"Well, we kind of went along with the sister telling us to follow her boyfriend's instructions."

"Which were?" Tony shuffled in his chair, his impatience beginning to show.

"To bury him at sea."

Tony looked at the man. "Is that unusual? I thought it happened now and then."

"Only if you report it. We did tell the sister about the death but she said too much was at stake to tell the authorities. We had to get rid of the rotting body, so we decided to do a burial right there. We were back in this part of the Gulf by then.

"We thought we'd better wrap him in something, but we didn't want to give up our sheets to make a shroud. And we needed the tarp. That's when he gave us his old raincoat."

"Who did?"

"Rolando."

"That's all? Just Rolando?"

The man shrugged. "He never told us a last name. I guess Bernard knew it."

"He gave you his raincoat, and?"

"We planned on wrapping Bernard in it like it was a shroud. It was big enough to tie the sleeves together with his arms in it. We used his belt and some rope to make sure his entire body was secure. Then we got an old anchor we no longer used and tied a rope to it and around his waist. We didn't want him to go floating off somewhere."

Tony dropped his head. I couldn't see his face, but I knew he was stifling a laugh.

"And did you say a blessing or something."

"Yeah, my buddy did. And Rolando shoved him into the water."

"He sunk?"

"Right away."

"And what did you think when you heard about the bones found in the river here?"

"Nothing. I didn't hear about it when you found them. Rolando did because he had come ashore. The sister was in a panic. I guess that's when he decided to pose as Bernard."

"His idea or hers?"

"Maybe both. I don't know."

"How soon did this happen after you pushed him, or had the burial at sea?"

"Months. Maybe eight."

"By that time, he'd been reduced to a skeleton, but his arms stayed inside the sleeves."

Tony must have said that for the sake of the recorder, but it made the man slump in his chair.

"Why, sir, did Marci not come forward at that point and declare it might be her brother?"

"Something about money. His sister needed the money that was coming to him and she was afraid it would stop otherwise."

"You can prove this?"

He shook his head. "No. It's just what Rolando told us. We didn't argue. We wanted to keep our jobs."

Tony asked the man to sit in the waiting area. He hadn't been charged with anything but if he tried to run, he would be. That's when the other guy spilled his guts in front of his maritime lawyer. It was nearly the same story, nothing that took a different angle.

He wasn't sure why Rolando became so important but figured it had to do with the sister.

"Do you think this Rolando was taking money off the sister?"

The man shrugged. Neither man seemed to know how much Marci was involved other than keeping her brother's death a secret.

"Nice lady," said Tony as he stood outside his office door.

Vernon winked at me and said, "Looks like that nasty little caterpillar in the middle has appeared."

"What are you talking about Drake?" Tony looked at him, realized it was a joke between us, and stomped inside to his chair.

"When is Long getting here?"

They had called Marshall Long to find out if the physical evidence could support the story they had just heard. He wasn't in the office when they called but on a journey to collect evidence from a stabbing at a bar.

"I may be big, but you still can't split me into two people," he said when he came into the office. "I've just seen a knife job done with the rustiest instrument the old guy could find in a dump. Why do drunks like to cut each other?"

"Maybe they think the other guy will bleed alcohol," said Vernon.

Tony shot him another glare. "I want you to listen to this man's story. Tell me the evidence supports what he says, please."

"Even if it doesn't?" Marshall said.

Tony motioned for him to sit in his chair, pointed to the PLAY button and left the room.

"It's the woman next," he said. "The sister. I need to question her about this dead brother thing."

"The lawyer is going to cry badgering his client on the other case," Vernon said.

"That's why we're getting the lawyer in here. We've got the story. When she knows that, she's going to have to say something in her own defense. That's when we find out if she's lying or she's going to cooperate."

"Is she back in her shop?" I asked.

"Nope. It's barricaded. We took pictures and will make copies for both sides. She's staying at a motel here in town, she said. We've got a phone number to reach her, and we've got a tail on her."

"And the other woman?"

"Tail on her, too. She was charged with assault, but made bail. Couldn't hold the two cohorts, but they've been warned to stay in touch."

"Let's hope the two women aren't in the same motel," said Vernon.

A deputy came into the hallway. He escorted a tall Latino man toward us.

"This is Mr. Rolando Rochinha," the deputy said. "He wants to make a statement."

CHAPTER TWENTY-FOUR

"Brazil, is it?" I asked the man standing next to Tony. "Or Portugal?"

"Brazil," he said. "But I grew up in the Keys. You won't get a word of Portuguese out of me."

"Not even an accent," I said and followed Vernon back inside the observation room. Marshall joined us, placing himself on a swivel chair that moaned and squeaked with his weight.

Tony asked if he wanted a lawyer since it was highly possible he'd be arrested.

"No," he said. "I know I impersonated someone, but that's all I did. I'll take my chances there."

"Impersonated in order to collect money."

"I didn't collect anything."

"But you helped someone else."

Rolando shrugged. "I can tell you what you need to know. Isn't that worth anything?"

Tony took a deep breath. He didn't promise anything, but sat back in his chair and said, "Start with how you met Marci Doucet."

"At the shop in New Orleans, before Katrina. I knew the owner, you see."

"Another of your lady friends?"

"I saw a bit of Miss Geurrin during that time."

"But Marci took over?"

"Are you going to let me tell this or not?"

Tony waved a hand for him to continue. He told how he had a few days off from a job on a ship and decided to visit his friend at her shop. Marci had been at the counter since Janine was at lunch.

"We got a little friendly, had some laughs for two days, and I had to leave. I didn't see her again until after Katrina. I ran into her at the docks in Mobile. That's when we started a sort of steady, shall we say visitation, when I was in port. When my job ended, she wrote to her brother, and he hired me."

"Tell me about the time right after Katrina, when Marci went back to the shop in New Orleans."

"She got into the area and found the place a mess. Much of the roof and one wall had caved in, and all the merchandise was wet. She said she had to wade in water up to midcalf."

"And the Guerrin woman, where was she?"

"No one knew. Marci said she gathered up anything that wasn't soaked and took it away in a friend's row boat."

"I heard there was money, too."

Rolando put his head down a moment, then faced Tony. "She had the key to the safe. It was waterproof so Marci opened it and found a lot of cash. Surprising how Janine would keep it there and not rescue it before the storm." He laughed a little.

"Marci never told me how much it was, but she kept it since she figured Janine was dead."

"Dead? She got away herself. Why would she consider her boss dead?"

"She couldn't locate her."

"Yeah, I'll bet she tried real hard, too."

Rolando claimed to not know where Janine was then or how

to find her. Marci ended up keeping the money and lots of stock that had been stored higher than the water line.

"Now tell me about Bernard Doucet."

Rolando related the story of the death and how Marci said to bury him at sea. Even the part about the burial shroud being his raincoat matched the story they had.

"She needed the money, you see. The ship would have been hers anyway, but she got the disability money, too. It just seemed convenient to let the world think he was alive."

Marshall Long twisted in his chair. He had heard enough.

"Tell Tony there is nothing in the coat or the bones to suggest someone killed the guy. Someone could have, mind you, but no one will prove it by the things we've got in the lab now." He stood, waved a salute to Tony as though he could see through the mirror, and left the room.

With Marshall back to his rusty knife killing and the Marci/Janine group in custody, it was time to exit and let Tony take care of the rest—Tony and the courts. Lawyers would be swimming in this one for months.

"I guess we can finally move out of the estate trailer," I said as Vernon drove me back to Ciel. "I really miss my house."

"You can clear out today if you want. The owner has found a new cash flow."

"He's renting to someone else?"

"A journalist has been following the events with the bodies, and he knows there is a river funeral happening soon. He wants to rent a spot, but he doesn't have his own trailer."

"He wants to soak up the refugee culture. That's what they are still, refugees. They never gave up their love of watery places. Not even the fear of a storm like Katrina could make them do that."

"Living on the edge of massive wipe out, I guess." Vernon turned to me. "You wouldn't move, either, would you?"

"Never," I smiled. "Even when the river overflows its banks and threatens to sit on my front porch. I can't imagine living where there is only barren dirt, rock, and sun."

"Even if they have rattlers in the desert?"

"Man cannot live on snakes alone, he must have mosquitoes."

"Speaking of funerals, what has Pasquin done about Jimpson's? I'm sure they're releasing the body soon."

"He's been planning it with his buddies. I'm not part of that, at least not until it actually happens. I'm waiting for instructions."

"We'll be following the procession in police boats. I think it may be a first."

We pulled into Kayleen's for a quick bite and to give her the news about her newly found lover who had just gone from being French to being Brazilian.

"I'm not all that surprised," she said. She sat across from us again, but her edginess was gone. "He was just a nice flash in the dullness, a momentary diversion, as they say."

"He may end up in jail," said Vernon. "You may end having to testify. What's Bub going to say?"

I knew what Vernon meant. He didn't know if Bub would resort to domestic violence.

"I told him," Kayleen said, her head lowered. "He kind of felt miserable, but he's back with his friends at the boat yard and doesn't even mention it. At least he's stopped harping about spending money now that he knows it's coming in, and I'm paying the bills."

I didn't dare ask about the soundness of that marriage. It had survived plenty of economic hardships and Katrina. Maybe it was comfortable and would last only under a different agenda.

Some couples are like that, no steam heat in the relationship but a lot of support in old, familiar boards. I laughed at myself for thinking in terms of a house. I wanted to be back there and right now.

"Oh, here's the man who is going to rent your trailer," said Kayleen as she looked up when the door opened. "He'll be here for a while because he's going to write some articles, maybe even a book, on life in this part of the state."

A man with lots of unruly hair that was graying at the temples stood at the door and looked around as though searching for someone. When he spotted Kayleen's waving hand, he smiled and came toward us.

"This is Joe Edmons," she said, almost blushing. "He's a journalist. These are the people who occupy the trailer for now."

We chatted with Joe for a while. He had a boyish grin with a dimple in one cheek. His lanky physique was tanned and healthy. There was no wedding ring. He knew how to infuse humor into the conversation, all the while asking questions for his journalistic work. He teased Kayleen, who blushed even more. She wasn't going to miss the handsome Rolando. The way he looked at Kayleen, Joe would make her the first of his research projects.

Vernon and I spent a couple of hours sorting out our things and packing them into the cars. After helping me settle the canoe atop the Honda, he had to get back to work. I drove by the shops before heading to my swamp house.

"You're leaving this first class hotel?" said Harold. "You'll come back now and then?"

"I'll be back and most likely with that other old man. You'll be down our way, too, I'll bet. He's known for his late night fetes."

"I've heard, but lordy, I cannot stay up past nine."

"You'll never make it in Cajun like that. Besides, you've got a boat and can go home early."

He shook his head. "No more. I sold it."

I waved goodbye and dropped in to do the same at Mo's.

"Been nice knowing you," he said as he shook my hand. He wasn't big on emotional stuff and went back to reading his newspaper. Just before I closed the door, I turned to look back at him. He was staring at me. He raised a hand in a half wave, almost startled that I had looked his way.

The Talisman had yellow tape over the door. I didn't look inside. Its future looked dim, and I wondered if Sheila had seen anything to hint of it in her readings. The feeling made sad until I shook it off, knowing you can't read the future of a shop in the cards.

When I pulled into the road that led to my familiar abode, I touched the holy shrimp that still rested beneath my blouse. I wasn't ready to remove it just yet.

CHAPTER TWENTY-FIVE

The funeral was on, and it would be bigger than anyone imagined. Just about all the boats in the swamp had offered themselves to Pasquin. He had taken on most of the planning, with his cronies and Mama giving him advice.

"We got his ashes this morning. Had the mortuary put them in a gator skin." Pasquin stood on his porch and showed off the gator hide that had been shaped into a kind of large canteen with a nozzle. The nozzle was plugged with a homemade stopper. The idea was to unstop the nozzle and pour out the ashes at the designated spot on the river.

I stood on the ground outside Pasquin's porch along with about twenty others, all with black arm bands, some with life jackets.

Vernon joined us.

"Police escorts are ready when you are," he said and pointed toward the landing in front of Pasquin's house. "It's getting crowded out there."

"Soon as the band gets here," he said and waved his hat at Vernon.

"Band?" I said. This was getting bigger all the time.

"Just some swamp boys. Been practicing since the—uh, death."

"Maybe you should call them."

I started to hand over my cell phone when someone yelled

from the river bank. "Band's here!"

Someone had given a parade map and line-up sheet to each boat runner. Pasquin would follow a police boat and lead everyone down the Palmetto River to the mouth of the river. Slow was the name of the game. Manatees were about, and the fear was that one of the boats would kill one on the very day Jimpson was honoring them with his ashes.

It took a while to get everyone loaded at the landing and in the designated line. I rode in the sheriff's boat with Vernon and another deputy. Pasquin would guide his boat right behind us with Mama and Harold sitting side by side. The alligator hide with the ashes perched on a pedestal someone had fixed up with grips to make sure Jimpson didn't take an early fall into the water.

Behind Pasquin was a long line of motorboats, piloted with rugged river men and crowded with people whose own boats were too unreliable to make a dignified trek down the river.

"Any boat stalls, everyone move around it," said Pasquin. "Just don't hit anyone."

Someone had commandeered a larger fishing excursion boat for the band. It had been loaned from the boat yard. Bub and Gibby sat inside the cabin. Fortunately, neither had command of the wheel. On deck, the mish mash band had a zydeco rub board and accordion along with a Cajun fiddle, a trumpet, and a bongo player. The bongo mostly beat out a rhythm on one instrument with one hand.

At the end of the boat line, the other sheriff's boat took a position and signaled Vernon to begin. He sounded the horn and started the engine.

Once the entire line moved up the river, the band began a slow, sad tune. They had no singer but I could hear a few boat people mouthing some words along with the music. Mama dabbed at her eyes. The bongo beat out a labored funereal rhythm. The trumpet and fiddle took turns with the melody, all done low key.

"Who rigged up the microphone on that thing?" I asked. The music could be heard all over the banks and far into the woods. Birds flew from tree tops that couldn't be seen from the water.

"Pasquin wanted it heard, and you know the sound won't carry on shore if there isn't a system."

Vernon maneuvered the boat around a cypress growth in the middle of the river. He outstretched both arms briefly to advise his followers to go around the barrier. Like pros, the boats parted, went around the cypress knee island and rejoined each other on the other side. The band never stopped playing.

"I don't think Jimpson ever spent a day in New Orleans," I said. "He's not Cajun. Would he have approved of his own funeral?"

Vernon had no answer for me. I never knew Jimpson like Pasquin did. Maybe the two had listened to this music together at one of the late night gatherings. Maybe it was just the only way Pasquin knew to send off the old fellow. I relaxed. Jimpson would like it. Had it been someone else who died, he would have been here like all the others.

The banks of the river were dotted with people watching our boat parade. Some placed hands or hats over their hearts. Others just stood on their expensive docks and stared at the spectacle. In a couple of places, television crews filmed us. And as they say, the band played on, its music recorded for the late news.

"Jimpson would have never thought his death would bring out the world," I said.

"Too bad it took a murder to do it."

"Do you think O'Neil is watching all this?"

"No," said Vernon. "But I understand they are watching O'Neil. Suicide watch."

"The man was so upset over his wife's impending death that he killed for her." It made no sense to me for O'Neil to give a dying woman one parting gift of a successful reading and having to murder to accomplish it.

"I've seen stranger motives," said Vernon.

The bridge near the bay opening came into view. Vernon raised one arm and blew the horn. Its shrill blast let the others know we were near the manatee habitat. The line of boats slowed to nearly a stop and seemed to drift beneath the bridge into the bay opening. Many of the occupants looked over the side and pointed to the big sea mammals moving close to the boats. The animals sensed no danger, it seemed. One came so close to the side of the sheriff's boat, I thought I could touch it.

"It's like they want to snuggle up to the vehicle," I said. "No fear of death at all."

"Like Jimpson," said Vernon. "I'll bet the man had waited on O'Neil several times. No idea he'd knock the life out of him."

I stared down at the manatee. It stuck with the boat, even when we stopped. It would be okay if it stayed on the side, but if it drifted beneath the propeller and stayed too close, it could take its place alongside Jimpson's ashes.

The band stopped playing and silence fell over the banks and the river. The crowd was larger here. I looked for Joe the journalist but he wasn't on the bank. He could have been on one of the boats.

"The sky is holding," I said. "Let's hope it keeps on holding for the fete."

"And let's hope the old guys can hold their liquor at that fete," said Vernon.

Mama had agreed to allow a memorial party to happen outside her restaurant in Fogarty Spring. The same band would sit on its boat at the landing and play for the mourners who would be both inside and on the grounds of Mama's Table.

But that would be later, after the procession turned and headed back up river. Right now was the small ceremony of ash strewing.

Vernon waved to Pasquin who steered his boat slowly around us and took a spot where the bay opened up wide, where ocean and river waters mixed in the swirling currents. His boat swayed a bit in the water movements, but Pasquin had chosen the right time of day for the calmest waters.

No one could really hear him, except Mama and Harold, but I knew Pasquin was going to say, "Adieu and goodbye, my friend," nothing else.

He held up the gator container and waved it toward the boaters who sent up a cheer. Turning to the side of his boat, he uplugged the stopper and let the ashes flow into the water. Pasquin even knew the winds of this time of day. He had positioned the boat at an angle to carry the ashes away from him and into the water.

When all the ashes had been strewed, Pasquin leaned over, his one hand grasping the side of his boat and Harold helping him balance. He filled the container with the water, swirled it around, and poured it out again. Replacing the stopper, he turned the container on its side and laid it back on the pedestal. Giving a nod to Vernon, he restarted his boat and moved back to his spot, heading upriver. All the boats waiting turned at that point, and the band struck up a lively tune. It was danceable and people in the boats were moving about as though they wanted to dance on water. People along the banks did jigs or applauded.

"This river has never seen such an event," I said. "Will it start a trend."

"Not sure about that," said Vernon. "But dying sure is a trend."

CHAPTER TWENTY-SIX

"Jimpson wasn't Cajun, but you sure gave him a Louisiana send off," I said. Harold, Pasquin, and I sat in the worn beach chairs that had become a permanent fixture outside the Oddities shop.

"Been six months in the water with the manatees," said Harold. "Think those creatures know he's down there with them?"

Pasquin sighed. "Not a bad place to be, really. I'd prefer he was back in his bait and tackle store, but down there with the fishes ain't so bad."

"Now how would you know?" asked Harold. He sipped on a giant bottle of soda.

"Don't. But haven't seen any fishes departing the territory. Must like it." He turned to his new friend and laughed his old man throaty sound. He held a bottle of soda, too, and tipped it toward Harold. "Here's to the Jimpson."

I smiled and looked at the sky. Summer and hurricane season had ended. It would be another five months before the threats came from Atlantic disturbances off the coast of Africa. Most days had a slight chill in the air, but out of the wind, the Florida sunshine still warmed a soul.

I had moved away from Ciel, both in body and spirit, since the funeral. My goddaughter, Sissy, had returned from dive camp, knowledgeable enough, she thought, to tackle some caves. It bothered me, and I spent Saturday mornings trying to convince her to take it slower. So far, I was successful, but I knew—just as I knew myself as a small girl—that the daredevil would push herself to the dark and dangerous soon enough.

"Who is that?" I said as I saw a strange woman walking toward the shop where The Talisman used to be.

"Oh, that's Belinda Cardel," said Harold. He chuckled and Pasquin made it a duet. "She's bought that shop and is keeping up the tradition."

I heard the sprite tinkle over the door. Janine hadn't managed to destroy that.

"Another fortune telling shop?" I asked.

"Yeah. She's got three readers lined up out of that crowd Miss Doucet was interviewing to replace Sheila."

"But, what has she done to her hair?"

"Dyed it black!" Pasquin gave his knee a slap with his straw hat. "Makes her look like a witch." He and Harold laughed again.

I wandered toward the shop. The door wasn't locked. I took a chance and let the sprite announce me.

"We won't be open for another week," said Belinda.

"I'm just curious," I said. "Is it going to be another shop like The Talisman?"

I looked about. The floors had been cleaned of any glass and debris from the fight. Maybe some of the merchandise was the same—it looked as though it was—but it was nicely displayed with printed cards explaining its magic.

"And you'll have readings?"

Belinda moved into the light coming from the front window. Her dyed hair was shoe polish black. She had used mascara around her eyes and powder over the rest of her usual ruddy complexion. If witch was her goal, she was going through the zombie stage first. She wore shorts and a tee shirt today. I pictured her in black scarves for opening day.

"Yes, but not only Tarot. We have three mediums, one for Tarot, one for palms, and one mental medium."

"What's a mental medium?" It sounded made up to me, but then most of this stuff sounded that way to me.

"She can look at your aura and eyes and such, and tell you things."

"I see." I didn't see much except dollar signs, of course. "And you'll run the shop?"

"Yes. I'm taking classes in herbs right now. I plan to be the expert around here." She smiled.

"Your husband would be proud." I'm not sure why I said that. It wasn't to be cruel, but maybe to find out how all this happened. Belinda didn't take it as an affront.

She shrugged. "He had good insurance. I bought a new car and this shop." She looked at me after a moment of hesitation. "I also bought Miss Doucet's trailer after I sold my house. I'm moving in this weekend."

I nodded, not knowing what to say. I was tempted to quote the Bible, "and the meek shall inherit the earth," but thought that might be out of line. No religion was rejected in a place like this. It all fit into the realm of spiritual contact.

"And will the place keep the same name?"

"Oh no. I'd never do that. The former name has bad vibes." She moved behind the counter and brought out a poster. "This is the sign painter's rendering of the one he'll put over the door."

THE WATER WITCH in black letters over swirls of wave-like blue paint stared back at me.

"I'll keep the sprite. She survived the melee and will be a good omen."

Belinda lit a bit of incense on her counter. Spying a box of unwrapped crystals, I remembered the bookends. They never made it to Kayleen's counter. It seemed a bit outrageous to have them sitting in Rolando's one-time lover's place of business. They were sitting in my hall closet in the old Talisman bag. Maybe I'd take them to my office in the linguistics department, something to remind me of my other life. Giving the place one last look, I drifted back to the old men.

Mo had joined Pasquin and Harold. He jumped up when I came and dragged a stool out for himself. The four of us sat and watched the bay, its waves moving closer with the tide.

"Kayleen is doing well," I said. "Now you've got a new magic shop. A convenience store and an oddities store. Not to mention publicity enough to fill up the fish camp and bring tourists all weekend. What else could you want?"

The men sat quietly until Harold spoke. "Two of us know it's temporary," he said, his voice void of the humor he had used on Belinda's venture. "See the way this bay curves around and comes in from the open ocean? It's prone to flooding if a storm hits west of here. The surge will come in fast and furious. Worse if it's high tide. Not a thing, shops, café, camp—it will all be under water. All this junk will wash out there."

"Then what?" asked Pasquin.

Silence sat over us like a dark cloud until Harold spoke up again.

"Then I'll collect all the washed up junk and put it up for sale." He laughed, and we joined him until a roll of thunder made us jump and run for cover.

Recommended Memento Mori Mysteries

Other books by Glynn Marsh Alam:

RIVER WHISPERS

Luanne Fogarty Mysteries
DIVE DEEP and DEADLY
DEEP WATER DEATH
COLD WATER CORPSE
BILGE WATER BONES
HIGH WATER HELLION
GREEN WATER GHOST
MOON WATER MADNESS
(Florida Book Awards: 2009 Gold Award Winner)

Glynn Marsh Alam is a native Floridian. Born in Tallahassee, she is familiar with the live oak forests and cypress swamps of the area. She also knows the sinkholes and reptilia that abound there. She often swims in the cold, clear springs above the openings to fathomless caves. These are the settings for her Luanne Fogarty mystery series (*Deep Water Death, Dive Deep and Deadly, Cold Water Corpse, Bilge Water Bones, High Water Hellion, Green Water Ghost*) and for her literary novel, *River Whispers*.

After graduating from Florida State University, Glynn worked as a decoder/translator for the National Security Agency in D.C., then moved to Los Angeles where she taught writing and literature and earned an MA in linguistics. After many years of traveling back to Florida twice a year, in 2004 she moved there and writes full time.

Visit Glynn Marsh Alam at www.glynnmarshalam.com.